Old Well

Old Well

BY ZHENG YI

Translated by David Kwan
Introduction by Anthony P. Kane

San Francisco

Cover illustration and design by Robbin Henderson
Cover photographs from the film, Old Well *(Lao jing), directed by Wu Tianming*

This edition copublished with Panda Books, Beijing China

Library of Congress Catalog Card Number: 89-60882

ISBN 0-8351-2275-1 (casebound)
ISBN 0-8351-2276-X (paperback)

Printed in the United States of America by & Periodicals, Inc.

Contents

Introduction

Revolutions are meant to solve problems, and the Chinese revolution solved quite a few. It reunited a country that had been disintegrating from within and torn apart from without for over a century. When Mao Zedong proclaimed the establishment of the People's Republic of China on October 1, 1949, it meant that for the first time since the Opium War, China was free of all foreign control. Not since the collapse of the Manchu empire in 1911 had the country been united under one government. China had stood up as a modern nation-state for the first time in history, and as Napoleon had predicted, it truly astonished the world.

But while the Chinese revolution solved those basic problems of national sovereignty and unity, it still had to cope with massive poverty, the damage done by the long war with Japan, and the legacy of traditional culture. Rural China remained (in the words of Mao himself) "poor and blank." In the Korean War the Chinese proudly fought the world's greatest superpower, the United States, to a standstill, but even after a three-year program of national reconstruction and massive redistribution of wealth through land reform, China remained an underdeveloped nation, part of the "third world." Victory in the struggle to modernize the new China would prove even more difficult to achieve than it had been in the hard-fought battles already won.

After completing land reform in the countryside and taming crime and inflation in the cities, the country's new leaders moved immediately toward "the transition to socialism" with the introduction of a Soviet-style five year plan for the economy. In the factories this meant a Stalinist emphasis on heavy industry at the expense of consumer goods. In the countryside it meant a process of collectivization beginning with mutual-aid teams and ending in large agricultural cooperatives by the mid-fifties. Peasants perhaps sometimes joined rather reluctantly, out of respect for Chairman Mao. But when this form of collectivization failed to produce the agricultural surpluses necessary to pay for industrialization (and as relations with the Soviet Union soured after Stalin's death and denunciation), Chairman Mao decided that the country was ready for a sudden leap into communism.

The Great Leap Forward, introduced in 1958, forced people into communes, effectively depriving the peasants of the control over their land and their destinies which they had won from oppressive landlords only a short time before. In their haste to answer the Chairman's call to develop sideline rural industry, peasants built millions of "backyard furnaces" to produce steel for the cities. The steel proved worthless and the crops rotted unharvested in the fields. Bad weather followed manmade disaster, and millions of Chinese starved. Mao was forced to resign as head of state in 1959, but he refused to acknowledge that his plan had failed on its own merits.

Convinced that his ideas had been undermined in their implementation by "capitalist roaders" in the Chinese Communist Party, Mao began a comeback that climaxed in the launching of the Great Proletarian Cultural Revolution in 1966. Using a cult of personality and his tremendous influence in the People's Liberation Army, Mao called upon the nation's youth to become his "revolutionary successors" and attack the "demons and monsters" who had taken over the Party from within. Millions of "Red Guards" answered the Chairman's call, traversing the country in "long marches" and attacking the influences of both the feudal past and the bourgeois west. Often those who had been praised as last week's heroes were attacked as this week's villains. The country reached the brink of civil war before Chairman Mao reluctantly called in the People's Liberation Army to restore order.

In the end, the most difficult challenge for many revolutionary governments has been solving the problems created by the revolution itself. Mao Zedong perhaps provides history's greatest example of revolutionary success turned to bitter failure after the seizure of power was complete. The Great Leap Forward and the Cultural Revolution opened new wounds, wiping out earlier successes in the minds of younger Chinese-born after 1949 and leaving deep scars on virtually the entire population. The ideological fervor that swept the Chinese Communist Party into power had nearly led it and the nation to destruction twenty years later. In the process, the definitions of words like revolutionary, counterrevolutionary, and reactionary had become hopelessly blurred. China's post-Cultural Revolution leadership was to spend over a decade trying to undo the harm.

The Cultural Revolution was a disaster for China's development because it disrupted badly-needed education, demoralized millions of people, and wasted the energies of the masses in violence against each other, political bickering, and anti-intellectualism.

In time it became apparent that the excesses of repeated political campaigns had created an ideological and spiritual vacuum for people in all walks of life, including the Party cadres. Many saw the need for a return to more basic values, a blending of old and new, to resolve the crisis of belief. But it is a bitter irony that in the People's Republic of China today traditional attitudes and culture continue to be viewed by the authorities as a threat to their revolution. Aging veterans of the Long March and the Anti-Japanese War of Resistance hold fiercely to the belief that all non-socialist values are a threat to the revolution. The reformers trying to solve China's many economic, political, social and cultural problems ran with increasing frequency into very restrictive and dogmatic interpretations of the "Four Basic Principles": adherence to socialism, the democratic dictatorship of the people, the rule of the Communist Party, and the guiding ideology of Marxism-Leninism-Mao Zedong Thought. A hundred flowers could bloom, as long as the gardeners could continue to paint the roses red.

This was the harsh lesson that a number of aging Communist Party leaders came out of retirement to deliver to the Chinese people in Tiananmen Square on June 4, 1989 and in the weeks and months that followed (no sign of a letup has appeared at the time of this writing). Although they railed against the influence of foreign values with epithets like "spiritual pollution" and "bourgeois liberalization," they were equally opposed to any exploration of values from China's pre-revolutionary past. Even those Chinese leaders who sought to find answers in socialism were ultimately deemed traitorous, for the conservative government refused to acknowledge that the revolution created any new problems or that it might need some help in solving those that remain.

While most Americans became aware of these problems only recently, many Chinese thinkers had seen a crisis coming for years. The author of *Old Well,* Zheng Yi, is keenly aware of the contradictions, the clashing ideas, and the complexity of modern China. Born in 1948 into a well-educated and elite family which was viewed with some suspicion by the Communists, Zheng was privileged to attend the best schools. Yet he strongly identified with the working class and even took up boxing as a way of stamping himself as a rugged friend of the common people. In spite of this sympathy for the poor and his early enthusiasm for the Party, he was denounced during the Cultural Revolution and once nearly beaten to death by a friend who turned on him at that time.

At the dawn of the Cultural Revolution, however, he was still a student of architecture at prestigious Qinghua University. Perhaps if fate had taken a different turn, he would have ended up as a professional architect who secretly entertained the hope of becoming a writer. What happened instead was that he survived several years of hard experience as a farmer, shepherd, and roaming laborer in northern China. Crossed by "China's sorrow," the mighty Yellow River, this vast territory was the historic cradle of Chinese civilization. But made barren by several millennia of human activity and ecological abuse described in *Old Well,* it is now one of China's poorest areas, a stark symbol of the struggles of the Chinese people as a whole to overcome their relative backwardness and flourish once again. The authenticity of his descriptions of rural China results from his having worked side by side with peasants, physically sharing the incredible hardships in the countryside.

Some of his observations made during this period were also revealed in his other major novel, *A Village So Far*, a disturbing account of the twisted sexual psychology of the people in a region where men are forced to share wives because of extreme poverty.

Zheng's writing is quite distinct from some other Chinese works with similar themes, in that his perspective is relatively free of the normal trappings of self-pity, sentimental indulgence, and melodrama. The serenity with which he approaches the harsh lives of his characters reveals, paradoxically, a greater and more universal kind of compassion, and an ability to transcend the considerable sense of suffering and bitterness which people acquire from harsh experiences. The result is a degree of maturity and sophistication in his work thus far matched by very few of his contemporaries.

His literary form and his treatment of moral dilemmas show a decisive Western influence. But the smell and color of the heaving yellow earth permeates every line in the novel, and the rich colloquialism and folk customs (which unfortunately are difficult to convey in translation) make the story deeply Chinese. It is this literary ability to convey the feelings of China and her rural people that gives *Old Well* its power. Aside from providing the kind of political and sociological insights into issues discussed here, the book is a compelling piece of fiction. The tragic feeling in the novel has historical and even ecological roots, yet it is just as much a tragedy of love. Underneath the specific social problems presented are the powerful currents of love, anger, pride, and compassion: the forces that provide the basic emotional energy necessary for authentic literature in any culture.

Old Well is also significant to the cinema in modern China. Nowhere was the irony of the Chinese Communist Party's self-created predicament more profoundly appreciated than in the films produced in the mid-1980s at the Xi'an Film Studio under the leadership of producer, director, and studio chief Wu Tianming. From Chen Kaige's *Huangtudi* (Yellow Earth), released in Hong Kong in 1985, to Zhang Yimou's *Hong gaoliang* (Red Sorghum), a centerpiece of the 1988 New York Film Festival, films produced at the Xi'an studio share a deep appreciation for life in the barren plains of China's northwest.

We have Wu Tianming to thank for bringing *Old Well,* to international attention. The film, *Lao jing,* which Wu directed himself, won the top prize at the Tokyo International Film Festival. Although criticized at home and given virtually no commercial distribution, the film's international acclaim focused attention both on its director and on Zheng Yi. Much of what was controversial about the film comes out of Zheng Yi's eloquent and wrenching story about Old Well Village's long struggle for survival in the face of a disappearing water supply. It is a struggle to revitalize a wounded land, a struggle made more difficult by man's self-destructive ability to magnify the destructive power of nature by upsetting its delicate balance.

But that, of course, is the value of the story for the Chinese reader, and the nature of the threat it poses to the authorities. The story does not blame the Party's leadership for the harshness of life in drought-stricken Old Well—this is an agony inherited from the past—but it does question the Party's relevance in addressing problems that survived unnoticed in far-away Beijing. The "real" world outside the capital, the world of northern Chinese village life portrayed in *Old Well,* is not a simple place where people born on the land are pure of heart and troubles are always caused by foreign influences. The challenges facing the people of Old Well Village are challenges created by the forces of nature and human history, forces which at times can be harmonized but which at times clash violently with each other.

The Chinese Communist Party is only a recent player in the history of the Chinese people's struggle to feed themselves on a relatively small plot of arable land. (China is roughly the same size as the United States, but its population is nearly five times as large and the percentage of arable land is considerably smaller.) The Party's ability to continue to play a role in the struggle depends on its ability to integrate itself into the landscape. In challenging the Party to become a part of the struggle, the author is clearly not intending to challenge its authority; rather, he is exposing a challenge to man's existence on the harsh land that any would-be leader must face and overcome. The importance of that struggle is symbolized in the story by the haunting discovery of a cave once used by the Eighth Route Army, the pre-1949 precursor of the People's Liberation Army. The Japanese enemy was defeated at the cost of many lives, the author seems to be saying, but the struggle to survive today is just as important and every bit as much a struggle of life and death.

As is often the case with modern Chinese literature, *Old Well* finds itself trapped between the artistic conventions of China and the West. The Chinese reader is instantly struck by the sexual frankness and directness of the story, personified by the female protagonist Zhao Qiaoying. An outsider who by "a mean trick of fate" was conceived in the city but born in rustic Old Well, Qiaoying shocks Chinese sensibilities from the beginning by begging her high school sweetheart, Sun Wangxuan, to marry her and take her away from the village. These "modern" attitudes are naturally associated with values imported from the West.

Yet the city is also a symbol of a materialism alien to the "innate qualities of the country girl" that are at Qiaoying's core, a materialism that in her mind, at least, (and can the reader disagree?) is equated with communism. Her goal is simply to learn scientific agriculture in order to improve the lives of her fellow villagers, and yet to accomplish the goal she must overcome traditional inhibitions against women receiving an education and working outside the home. From the typical villager's point of view, her "communist" career goals are as foreign as her "western" lifestyle and dress. They are goals incompatible with the still existing feudal and patriarchal attitudes toward women, which persist in spite of the revolution.

Wangxuan, the story's hero, is more traditional than Qiaoying but equally complex, yearning to break free of the family ties that bind him to the village's founders of nearly a thousand years ago. The reader is introduced to the village's history early on, a history in which Wangxuan's ancestors had given up their lives in the quest for water, and Wangxuan can break free of it only by making it live again by finding water for his once fertile but now parched village. Along the way he embraces the communist system by taking an official post, but any Chinese reader sees this as an ironic anomaly. His decision to sacrifice his personal desires for the good of the village and out of respect for his grandfather reflect traditional Confucian values. The well he seeks to dig may be made possible in part by modern geological science with the help of Party officials, but it ultimately becomes a symbol to Wangxuan not of the communist present but of continuity with the past.

It is only when Wangxuan violates traditional values by continuing his affair with Qiaoying that he in any way resembles the "communist" man of new China. Or that is at least one way the author invites us to construe Wangxuan's daring defiance of the "feudal" practice of having been "bought like a slave" by his wife's family. Thus it is the night he spends in a cave with Qiaoying that leads directly to his appointment as Party branch secretary of the village. Ironically, this leadership position has nothing to do with typical moralistic communist values expounded by the Party's ideologues who remain puritanical. Nor, for that matter, are his inner struggles related to "revolutionary" versus "counterrevolutionary" values. He, like Qiaoying, shocks both traditional *and* Party sensibilities with his sexual behavior, embracing simultaneously the security of his wife and son and the passions of his illicit love for Qiaoying. Shortly after becoming Party secretary, he declares a holiday to allow the villagers to hear a bawdy performance by a band of traveling minstrels. The village elders approve of the move, welcoming the troop with gifts of tea and cigarettes. But the incident eventually leads to a scandal and an investigation by the Ministry of Culture. (In the film version of *Old Well,* Wu Tianming shows his own sense of irony by choosing the role of the cultural commissar to make a Hitchcock-like cameo appearance.) The irony is inescapable here. One reasonable Party official makes it possible for people to enjoy themselves in a seemingly innocent activity, only to be attacked by another authoritarian and puritanical Party bureaucrat.

Sexual passion, moral ambiguity, and human complexity all lie at the heart of *Old Well.* To a readership raised on the ideological campaigns of the Anti-rightist Movement, the Cultural Revolution, and now the campaign against "bourgeois liberalism," all of these factors point to an author influenced by the alien literary values of the modern West. Yet as noted, the context of the story is distinctly Chinese; its value for both the western and the Chinese reader is the forcefulness with which the author shows the pervasiveness of traditional values in a rapidly changing world.

Indeed, if there is a single message in *Old Well,* it is that the modern world is far too complex for any set of simple solutions to apply. Traditional values may rise at times from senseless superstition, but they also offer spiritual comfort in difficult periods. Or so it is argued in the musings of Party cadre Sun Fuchang when he is presented with a plot to steal the Dragon King from a neighboring village, a plot to which he eventually gives conditional support. When Qiaoying later chides the villagers for trusting in "tricksters and necromancers from the outside" to find water when other villages have had the good sense to rely on Wangxuan, it is this outburst that finally galvanizes the fundraising campaign that in turn leads to the final, successful sinking of a well for the village. Only the combination of young and old, modern and traditional (and yes, wife and mistress!) is capable of forging the final victory in this epic, multi-generational struggle for survival.

Anthony P. Kane
New York
October 1989

Chapter 1

Deep in the Taihang Mountains is a river called the Qinglong. An insignificant river at first, it grows and gathers strength as it battles its way out of the wilderness, impatient to join the placid River Fen. Just before it reaches its rendezvous on the loess plain, the river slows. Exhausted by its headlong dash, it hesitates, lingers, meanders in long lazy loops round the foot of the last mountains. At a bend of one of these loops, set in a valley between the river and the mountains, is a village called Old Well.

The light of day had barely burned through the dank mist when a young woman came out of the courtyard next to the only well with a workable winch in the east end of the village. Her hair was done up in a square of colored cloth, and across her shoulder she carried a pole from which two iron pails hung, one in front and the other behind. The pails squeaked and swayed as she walked.

During the night there was a spattering of spring rain—just enough to moisten the parched earth so that the mountains, rocks, trees, fields gone to seed, and the village itself sparkled in the pale light.

Somewhere in the courtyard a door squeaked, and a man was heard coughing inside.

"Are you going to the back well, Qiaoying?" the man asked.

"Yes father." The young woman did not slacken her pace.

"But there won't be much water." The man's voice sounded annoyed.

Enough for two pails, at any rate, thought Zhao Qiaoying. She squared her shoulders and continued up the slope. The winter had been without snow, and the spring rains were late. The river was down to a trickle, and the wells were dry. As long as there was some rain you could get a pail or two of brackish water out of the wells. But it had been dry too long, and the only water was in wells five and ten li away. Still, one would have to start out at the first light before sunrise and fight for a couple of pails of water that would have to last out the day. Carrying water was a chore Zhao Qiaoying hated.

What was called the back well was really a hollow in the pebbly bed of a dried up stream. Water collected in it after a shower. The back well was only a little over a li from the village, and just as Qiaoying thought, there was water in it. She set down her pails, took up the ladle she had put in one of them and began scooping up water. She filled her pails, then filled the ladle again. She untied her kerchief, soaked it, and pressed it wringing wet to her face, shivering deliciously as the stinging cold water trickled down her nose, cheeks and chin.

It is said that cattle die of thirst in Old Well Village because there is no well, and after nine droughts in ten years water is as precious as oil. But the people of Old Well become philosophical when they speak of their lack of water. They claim the water they use to wash their faces is used again to wash yams. After that it is given to the pigs. Their neighbors who live close to the river banks scoff at the mountain folk saying that when a mountain family rises in the morning, they form a circle round the head of the family, who takes a mouthful of water, spins on his heels, and blows it into the faces gathered around him. That is called a face wash. Although an exaggeration, it is not far from the truth. Mountain folk seldom wash their faces. A man will get a wash every time he goes to the barber. The women, who carry the water and do the washing, clean themselves more frequently.

Qiaoying's face glowed after a good scrubbing. It was a typical mountain girl's face. There was a hint of stubborn pride in the slender, slightly upturned nose. Her clothes came from the city.

She wore a light blue jacket with wide lapels over silver-grey slacks. The tops of a red sweater and the snowy white collar of a blouse showed through the neckline of her jacket. On her feet were a pair of wine red leather pumps with half heels. Her long lustrous hair was pulled back from her face and tied with a bright ribbon. Zhao Qiaoying was not a country girl; at least not in her own eyes. Being conceived in the city and born in a place like Old Well was a mean trick of fate. Her parents had been caught in the three years of turmoil when urban populations were thinned out by uprooting thousands and transplanting them in far off places. In Qiaoying's mind communism and materialism were the same thing. And the city was the epitome of materialism. She longed for life in the city. She dreamt of escaping the village, yet she feared leaving too. For underneath the citified veneer she carefully cultivated were the innate qualities of the country girl which would ultimately expose her for the impostor she was. It was exposure of her origins that held her back. In Old Well she stuck out like a sore thumb. But she had gone to high school in the city and brought back scientific ideas of agriculture that actually worked. She was admired for that. Nevertheless it was generally felt that when it came to settling down, only a man from the city would do.

Qiaoying sat on a rock, her face tilted to the early morning sun. She untied her hair, letting the wind play through it as she combed. She did not notice the large brownish animal creep out of the underbrush behind her until it stuck its snout into the water, on the opposite side of the hollow, lapping noisily. Qiaoying wheeled about and gazed into the baleful yellow eyes of the beast. It was thin and very thirsty. She stamped her foot and shouted at the animal. It stood its ground, giving a deep rumbling growl, snapping its fangs, its long bushy tail waving menacingly.

"Wolf" flashed through Qiaoying's mind. She backed away from the hollow and ran up the path, tripping and sliding as she went. A shoe was torn from her foot. She plunged on blindly, her breath coming in short painful gasps. As she reached the crest of the path, a man carrying a large slab of rock on his back was coming slowly down the mountain side.

"Brother Wangquan!" she cried.

A muffled response came from under the stone slab.

"Wolf . . . " gasped Qiaoying as she hobbled toward the man.

The man stopped and straightened, easing the stone slab slowly to the ground. He was young, taller than he first appeared. His close cropped head seemed small on his wide shoulders. His face and hard muscled body were burnt a deep brown by the sun. His large black eyes swept the stillness around them.

"Where?"

"The back well." She threw her arms around him, her face pressed tightly against his bare chest. He pushed her aside roughly, and bounded down the path to attack the wolf.

Qiaoying limped behind him as best she could.

She found him beside the hollow, dazedly holding half of her carrying pole, which had broken in two. A thin trickle of blood oozed from a cut on his forehead. She dabbed at the wound with a handkerchief, looking around nervously.

"It got away." He gave her a lopsided grin, and threw down the splinter of the carrying pole. "It wouldn't have if the pole hadn't broken."

Wangquan grabbed her arm and forced her to sit on a blue rock near the water hole before she could say a word. Then she saw the wolf again, limping toward the water. She screamed, and Wangquan held her with one arm and covered her mouth with his other hand.

The wolf froze with panic, but when it saw the water in the pit it could not help dragging itself over to wet its tongue. Suddenly, Wangquan let go of Qiaoying, charged at the wolf and leaped on him at full speed. Before she could get up, Wangquan and the wolf were fighting and rolling on the rocky ground.

"Rock, rock," Wangquan shouted, trying to strangle the wolf with both hands locked around its throat. Qiaoying rushed, picked up a rock and handed it to him. He pounded the wolf on the head until it gave up its struggle. Then he sat on the blue rock again, throwing his stone weapon away.

"Hai!" Qiaoying took a deep breath and sat close to him. Grasping his arm, she put her cheek on his shoulder, saying "You're so great. You killed it in no time."

Nothing is great. It was too thirsty to get away," he said with a dry smile. "No rain through the spring season. These animals are so thirsty. Not even afraid of people any more."

She said nothing, her fingers touching his face, moving tenderly across his forehead, tears in her eyes. He caught her hand roughly in his calloused one, and drew her closer.

"Sit awhile," he said huskily. They sat on a large boulder, not speaking.

Wangquan lit a cigarette and smoked moodily. She leaned against him, anxiously gazing around her. Every little sound made her jump. The rocks and the underbrush had become threatening and the silence oppressive.

She nudged her chin against Wangquan's shoulder. "I hate this place," she said under her breath. "Wangquan, let's get out together!"

The battered wolf struggled to stand up and did all it could to crawl several steps until it plunged its head into the water and then straightened its legs. Blood trickled from its mouth and spread quietly across the water.

Looking at the dead wolf, Qiaoying's black, almond-shaped eyes filled with tears. "See, it wasn't willing to be a thirsty ghost at the gate of hell." Then she turned her face and continued in an intimate tone as she looked at him. "Brother Wangquan, let's find a way to leave this place."

"I can't put it into words," Wangquan threw down the cigarette butt and said sadly. "It's hard to leave a native land where we have been rooted for so many years. Shit, another one's coming." He arched his back and picked up another rock.

A small animal ran through the rocks and then escaped behind a blue boulder, where it poked its head out to look around.

"Fox, a little fox," said Qiaoying, who hurried to grip his hand and then continued, "Let's go back. Don't bother it and let it have some water. It's so thirsty."

Looking at the water in the hole mix with the dead wolf's blood, Wangquan picked up the buckets, went to the hole, and pushed the blood back with his hands to clear the water where he dipped the buckets to fill them. He started to walk on with the full bucket, but stopped, laughing. "So that's why villagers call you 'fox spirit'—you are always on good terms with foxes."

"Well," Zhao Qiaoying answered, smiling at him, "I myself don't even know why I like these little animals so much and why they're not afraid of me either." She smiled and went toward the yellow fox, which was bending its head and wetting its tongue. The fox looked warily at the dead wolf and started to drink. Then, startled by Qiaoying, it turned to run.

"Hah, my baby, don't go away!" Qiaoying said as if talking to a child.

The little fox stopped and turned its head, looking straight at her. Qiaoying squatted down by the water and waved her hand, talking softly, "Come on, my baby. Come on and have a good drink of water. Nothing to worry about. You don't remember me? I'm Qiaoqiao."

Looking at the water first and then Qiaoying, the fox came back, bold, and began drinking and even let Qiaoying pet him in slow strokes.

Wangquan watched, amazed, mouth open. Zhao Qiaoying jumped back, and stood in front of him, like a child, saying, "Hah, now you should believe me."

"Fox spirit," Wangquan answered, not knowing what else to say. He stood abruptly, picked up the water pails and began to stride up the path.

Qiaoying hurried after him. After a few paces, Wangquan spotted a woman's shoe. He poked at it with his foot.

"These aren't fit for working in," he laughed.

Qiaoying blushed. She slipped on her shoe. Suddenly she was angry.

"Nobody tells me what to do," she answered, stamping her foot. "You're not my man and I'm certainly not your woman!"

A blank, hard look came into Wangquan's eyes. He started up the path again without another word. Qiaoying struggled to keep up with him, silenced by the grim look on his face. They walked in angry silence to where Wangquan had left his slab of stone.

It was a large slab of stone. Larger, in fact, than Qiaoying realized.

"Is it for a roof?"

"It's for a kang."

"I suppose the stone for the walls and the roof of the new house is ready . . . "

He glanced at her suspiciously but kept silent.

"All you need is a woman to put in the new house," she remarked bitingly.

"It costs too much right now," he replied, matching her sour tone, "I'll wait."

Ever since he failed the university entrance exams and came home to Old Well, his father and grandfather had been trying to arrange a marriage. At first he objected. But before long the truth of the matter was brought home to him. Actually he had no choice in the matter. The young women thought to be suitable refused to have him. In spite of his education, he was still a peasant from a poor village. That was an inescapable fact of life. For a while the marriage plans were dropped. But recently he sensed something was stirring again. He neither questioned the whisperings nor did he object to them. He waited. As for Qiaoying, whom he had known since childhood, she was not merely someone to avoid, she was to be shut out of his consciousness. Her unabashed longing for the city put her beyond the pale.

Qiaoying glided the trim toe of her shoe across the stone slab.

"How heavy is it?" she groped for something to say.

"About three hundred catties."

Her eyes wandered from the stone slab to the misty crags of Qinglong range. There is no one like him in the village, she told herself. Cutting stone in the mountains at first light; carrying it down to the village; hastily swallowing a bowl of gruel, and off to work in the fields. The pole-vault champion she had known in high school had become a typical peasant, cutting stone to build a house for a bride. In her mind, Wangquan was as much a misfit as she. Fate had misplaced them both. The rush of tenderness she felt with such startling poignancy was no longer the comfortable companionship of their high school days school. It was desire now.

She gazed at him, with his broad shoulders and that small, trim head. He was brown; as brown and rugged as the mountains that spawned him. His open red jersey was so faded and patched that the words "Track and Field—He County High School" were barely decipherable. There was an ugly patch at the back of his head so calloused that the hair would not grow. It came from carrying stone slabs on his shoulders day after day.

Qiaoying remembered the first time Wangquan had come down the mountain carrying a slab of stone. He had walked the whole way without stopping. He leaned the stone carefully against a wall, then his knees buckled and he dropped to the ground unconscious. The stone was streaked with blood, and the back of his head was cut almost to the bone.

Afterwards when he was asked why he did it, Wangquan smiled wryly and said, "I had to prove something, to myself . . . "

In the short time since they were in high school together, Wangquan had become the pillar of his family. The boy had become a man, and she was feeling the unfamiliar stirring of womanhood.

She dabbed his sweat streaked face and also the ugly bald patch on the back of his head with a tiny handkerchief.

He moved his head aside, and caught her hand.

"Someone might see us," he mumbled.

"So let them." She covered his hand with her free hand, gently kneading the scars and the cuts. Heat rippled through them, from one to the other. Qiaoying lowered her eyes. She could feel her cheeks burning.

"People say we're in love," she whispered. It was neither question nor statement.

For a moment Wangquan said nothing. He turned his gaze down the slope to the village half hidden by mist and the smoke of cooking fires.

"Don't tease," he sighed, withdrawing his hand. "We' re not at school anymore. All that talk about romance . . . and love . . . that was just talk. You have your ambitions, and I have my life. Let's leave it at that."

He picked up the buckets and started off again.

"Who's playing the tease now?" Qiaoying cried. She leaped at him, wrestled a bucket from his hand and slammed it to the ground.

Wangquan put the other bucket down carefully.

"What's the matter with you?" he exclaimed. "The water . . . "

"I don't care! I don't care!" She hammered his bare chest with her fists.

All her pent-up feelings suddenly broke out. "Since we came home you've changed. All you think of is building a house and finding a wife. You avoid me. If it wasn't for the wolf, you would have ignored me." She was crying, clinging to him, her hot cheeks buried against his chest, sobbing uncontrollably.

"Wangquan . . . Wangquan . . . I want you so much . . . marry me . . . please . . . "

His arms went around her in spite of himself. The fires he thought were dead blazed as hotly as ever. She lifted her tear-streaked face to his. He did not move. She waited. Wangquan's heart was like a lump of lead. Qiaoqiao . . . Qiaoqiao . . . you are like the river that must find its way out of these mountains, he thought. And I must stay. Nothing can tie you to this miserable place. It's not your fault. Not mine, either.

He held her miserably, wordlessly.

Suddenly, from the foot of the hill came the sound of a man singing. Once it had been a pleasant voice. But it was worn now, quavering and cracked.

> Two lotus blossoms bloom together!
> Before you leave me, tell me when shall you return?
> When the sesame flowers are bluer than blue
> When shall I come again, but it won't be easy.

Someone was approaching. Wangquan tried to free himself but Qiaoying clung to him.

"It's your crazy second uncle," she whispered.

A ragged old man came up the hill. He wore a garland of willow branches on his head, from which tufts of dirty grey hair protruded like porcupine quills. As he drew near, he waved merrily at the two young people.

"What have you been up to?" he giggled slyly. Then suddenly turning serious, he asked, "Have you seen my Little Chou? I can't find her."

"She went up the hill," Qiaoying quickly answered.

The strange old man turned and stumbled up the hill.

Wangquan's insane second uncle was obsessed with sinking wells in his youth. He was once trapped underground for a day and a night. When they finally dug him out he had lost his mind. He was terrified of wells from then on. His entire life was blotted from his mind, except Little Chou, the girl he loved. He wandered the mountains looking for her, singing the songs of his youth. At times he would lie in the underbrush and listen to wind moaning through the gullies and the ravines.

Wangquan watched him disappear into the mountain, a pitiful outcast condemned to wander for the rest of his life. The memory of his uncle's doomed love for Little Chou sent a chill through Wangquan. He gently pushed Qiaoying away, reached for the bucket and walked quickly down the path.

The village floated up to him through swirls of mist and smoke stirred by a fretful wind. But the dreamlike landscape would soon dissolve when the mist lifted, and the hot dry wind blew off the mountain. Then the village would lose its enchantment and revert to its harsh brown reality. The river was a bed of white pebbles, traversed by the hot wind laying waste to everything that stood in its path. Only scrub pines and brambles, tufts of coarse grass and wild chrysanthemums clung to the mountainside, and the people who refused to die . . .

A song of the Taihang mountains, wild and passionate, echoed from peak to peak.

Bean stalk coiling round and round
I don't want to go—brother, brother come back.
Nowhere can the madder sink its roots.
Oh, how can we marry with no money . . .

Wangquan stopped and looked back. Far in the distance he could see the old man sitting on the crest of a hill, silhouetted against the sky.

Chapter 2

No one knows who founded the village of Old Well. There are no steles or other historical records of the event. Legend places it in the Song dynasty, almost ten centuries past. All that is known of the founder was his family name, Sun. Because he was the second son, he was called Sun Laoer. The village was named "The Well of Laoer's Wife," after a mysterious mountain woman believed to have had magical powers.

It was a time of great calamity. The Yellow River flooded, inundating what is now Hebei province. The fertile plains were swept clean. Pestilence followed on the heels of famine. Those who could, gathered up their belongings and ventured out in search of new land.

The Sun family consisted of an ailing mother and three sons, the father having long since died. The oldest of the three chose to remain to care for his mother, while Laoer and Laosan were encouraged to move away and find a more promising place. There was a saying in those times, "Better go a thousand li westward, than a stone's throw to the east. The population was dense and land was scarce to the east. But to the west lay Shanxi, Shaanxi, Inner Mongolia and Qinghai, where unclaimed land stretched from horizon to horizon. The vast wilderness was the hope of the poor and the dispossessed, and the westward migration began.

Before her sons left home, the old woman broke a clay pot into three pieces. To each she gave a shard, so that they might identify one another when they met again. Laoer and Laosan knelt and knocked their heads against the ground and bade farewell to their home and mother.

Laoer joined a group trekking westward, begging food as he went. The trekkers moved slowly, weak with hunger. Some sold their children for a measure of millet. When children could not be sold, they were abandoned by the wayside or left on the doorsteps of temples. The grass along the wayside was eaten first, then the bark was stripped from the trees. Bloated corpses littered the plains from Hebei to Shanxi. Those who remained pressed on. It was not until the Qinglong Mountains rose on the horizon that the trekkers found food again.

Finally Laoer reached the Taihang Mountains. For three days and nights he was lost in a forest. The green of pine and cypress, the shimmering of poplar and elms, the dazzling reds and yellows of maple and oak sheltered him. Rabbits and pheasants darted through the grass. Mountain goats, deer, wild boars, wolves and foxes wandered the mountainside. When he came to the banks of the Qinglong River he knew he had found his haven.

Laoer cleared some land and built a crude shack. This was the beginning of Old Well Village. Before long other settlers arrived: the Duans, the Lis, the Zhaos and the Wangs. At first they were hunters and fishermen and gatherers of wild fruit. Gradually they took over the land, staking their claims with colored flags. The forest was razed and turned into farmland. Even to this day, every year before the start of spring planting, farmers light bonfires, and form the characters meaning "well" and "farm" with the ashes in honor of their ancestors who cleared the land a thousand years before.

The settlement grew. Within a few years all the trees except a few groves had been cut down. As the settlers multiplied and prospered, the Qinglong River began to dry up. The climate changed, the mountains became arid, and water was scarce as gold. From the hard search for water came the legend of how Sun Laoer found a well for the village.

Sun Laoer climbed mountain after mountain looking for water. One day at noon, he arrived in front of a small house. The door creaked open and a young woman came out. Shouldering a carrying pole with a purplish-red bucket on each end, she walked toward a path scattered with flowers. When Laoer saw her with the buckets swinging, he followed her at a distance, keeping hidden. The woman did not go far before she reached a well. She began to draw water from the well. With the scorching noonday sun beating down, Laoer could not help going to the girl and asking for water.

"Sister, I am passing through. Could I have a drink of water?"

The woman said nothing.

The angry Laoer muttered to himself, "Yes or no, you'd better say something. Why don't you drop your bucket into the well."

The words were barely out of his dry mouth when the bucket did fall into the well. He regretted what he said. The woman smiled, talking to herself, "You've destroyed one of my morning glories!" She picked a purplish-red morning glory by the well and blew a puff of air on it. In an instant, the morning glory turned into a purplish-red bucket. She used it to draw another bucket of water from the well. Then she turned to Laoer and smiled. "Hey, drink your water!"

Now he looked at her closely, her oval face, delicate features, green blouse and pants. Noticing his stare, the woman lowered her face, blushing. Laoer's face also reddened as he squatted down and drank the water. After he had enough, he wiped his mouth with his sleeve and asked: "Why didn't you let me have the water to begin with?"

She stared at him, annoyed. "You don't know what's good or bad for you. The water is ice cold. But you are hot after a long walk. Drink sooner and you'll get cramps." She shouldered her pole and buckets, and left. Laoer gazed after her as she went to her courtyard, knowing he'd be the luckiest man in the world if he could marry her. But being from a poor family, he feared he couldn't be blessed with such good fortune. This thought put him in despairing mood and he sat down on the stone ledge of the well. Suddenly a strange sensation made him stand up and turn around. He saw he had made a deep print on the well stone he'd just sat on. He felt such a surge of energy that he gripped the stone well mouth tightly, lifted on the well with all his strength, and pulled it up with the water. He was so excited he put the well on his back and began walking. The woman came after him, crying, "You've stolen my well. How can I live by myself without a well?"

"I live alone too." He kept walking as he said this and did not turn around.

She cursed him over and over and kept shouting, "You criminal, you thief."

Laoer grinned and walked faster with the well on his back. The young woman followed closely behind him, cursing all the way. Finally, she became tired and silent, and even began to help Laoer carry the well. They were married the same night they returned to his village.

One generation followed another. The climate became so dry that even the legendary ancient well finally gave out. In the dry season the Qinglong River dwindled down to a trickle, and the water holes turned into hollows of baked clay.

The desperate settlers called in water diviners who were royally wined and dined. These charlatans took their time. After days of feasting they would announce that a source had been revealed to them in a vision. Then the whole village was mobilized to dig at the spot the water diviner had shown them. When the water diviners failed, the villagers resorted to necromancy. The necromancers had a saying: "Just as blood flows through a man's head, so must water flow through the top of a mountain."

Some used a compass to locate the source of water. Others had more scientific means at their command. A porcelain dish was placed in a three foot hole in the ground and left overnight. In the morning they examined the dew drops collected in the dishes. Large drops indicated that a large body of water lay not far underground, while small drops meant the exact opposite.

In this way the villagers sank a dozen useless dry wells. In the dry season, they had to cross the mountains and fetch water from wells ten li away. In the rainy season and in the winter when the mountain trails were impassable, the villagers collected rainwater or snow. The rainwater was often muddy. The villagers discovered that adding a pinch of alum or soybean flour made the silt sink to the bottom, making the water sweet and clear. Snow was swept into piles and melted over a fire. It was drinkable but slightly bitter.

Life became a constant struggle for water. Although they complained, the villagers clung stubbornly to Old Well. The thought of leaving was unbearable to them. Most often it was the youths who clamored to escape when there was a drought.

"If there is no water we can carry it in," was the oldtimers' reasoning, "but what would you do without food? Our forefathers came here because there was no food elsewhere. Here we have land enough for everyone. This is a suitable place for the poor."

Thus life continued, through the dynasties, from Song to Yuan, Ming and Qing to the present time, coalesced in a pattern of bitterness and despair.

* * *

All day a dry wind buffeted the Taihang Mountains. At dusk a mist rose, enveloping mountains and village in a cool bluish haze, lulling them into the somnolence of night with a promise of relief.

The lights of Old Well Village were specially bright that night. The thunder of drums and the clanging of cymbals announced that a play was to be given. The lights and the sound of drum and cymbal drew a steady stream of people to the temple square. A temple fair was a respite from the monotonous grind of daily life. After liberation in 1949, the gods were taken from the altars and the temples were allowed to crumble from neglect. But the temple fairs and the ritual plays remained. Only the audiences have changed. Once the performances were given for gods and man. Now the gods were gone. Only the elderly, middle-aged men and housewives watched. The young people milled around on the outer fringes of the crowd, out of reach of the lights, moving restlessly, watching and waiting, and finally pairing off. For this was the only socially acceptable setting in which young men and women could meet, and they made the best of it. Young men with a few coins jingling in their pockets, and a good cigarette dangling between their lips, tried to be nonchalant. Young women with clean scrubbed faces trailed wisps of perfume as they strolled by cracking melon seeds between their teeth. They were like brightly colored butterflies flitting through the crowd, until they settled beside some young man. Eyes would meet; hands reached out kneading and caressing; words were uttered in urgent whispers. The play on the stage was a blur to them. The real drama was unfolding in the darkness beyond the footlights and in the empty fields.

The curtain had already gone up when Sun Wangquan pushed his way into the temple square. The old people who came early clustered at the front of the stage, sitting on tiny stools, pieces of lumber, old bricks and rocks. Wangquan plunged into the crowd. His air of cold indifference was gone. His dark, narrow face was animated and his eyes flashed with excitement as he looked at the crowd. He had put on an almost new school uniform of blue polyester, and an old army cap was pushed far back on his head, hiding the ugly bald patch. It was the first time he had come to the temple fair since returning to Old Well. He deliberately avoided fairs, knowing that Qiaoying would be there. But since the day he carried water for her, all that had changed. The coals of first love—which he thought were dead—flared up again. He had been restless ever since. Then when Qiaoying passed his door earlier, and gave him a toss of her head and a wink, he knew nothing could keep him from the fair. Besides, there was something he had to tell her. The elders were plotting a marriage for him again. They did not come right out and tell him in so many words, but laid a bait for him instead. And he had almost taken it hook, line and sinker, but he managed to get away.

"Well, what a surprise!"

Wangquan looked up and saw branch secretary Sun Fuchang's oldest son, Sun Wangcai coming towards him. Sun Wangcai was wearing an old green army cap which never left him.

"Have a cigarette. They're Phoenixes."

Wangcai handed him a pack, Wangquan took one, and they lit up.

Like Qiaoying, Wangcai had also been a classmate of Wangquan. He was lazy. Because his father was a petty official, he did as he pleased. Wangcai suffered from a chronic fungus infection of the scalp, so his classmates nicknamed him "Egg Head." The name stuck and followed him back to Old Well after he failed the university entrance exams. Wangquan wasn't a friend of Wangcai. He took a few puffs of the cigarette and turned to go.

"Hey Wangquan, we're not in school anymore, so lay off the assistant monitor airs." Wangcai gave him a playful jab on the shoulder and winked. "So you've got it going with Qiaoying again.

Tell you the truth, I could do with a bit of that myself . . . Now don't get me wrong. I haven't got your luck. By the way, she said to look for her under the scholar tree."

It was a tradition among young people to pass messages through a go-between. The message confused Wangquan. He groped for a a suitable response but couldn't find the words. He grinned at Wangcai and headed for the old scholar tree, deliberately taking a roundabout route.

Qiaoying was waiting under the scholar tree. She beamed at him as he approached, and waved. She had tied her long hair with a white scarf, and an arrangement of ringlets curled around her ears and temples. She wore a bright red blouse cut in western style, all the more eye-catching among the drab blues, grays and blacks.

"You look so western," Sun Wangquan blurted out the first thing that came to mind. Then seeing how the corners of her mouth turned down, he added lamely, "It seems a bit out of place."

"It's for you. I thought you might like a bit of color . . . but all you've got eyes for are rocks and dirt." She put her arms around him and hugged him tightly.

"Do you like my perfume?"

Wangquan wanted to push her away but could not. He looked around. A short distance away, a young woman stood staring straight at him. Beads of sweat broke on his forehead.

"Qiaoqiao . . . " he whispered. Though he smiled, there was a pleading note in his voice which she caught immediately. Qiaoying made a face at him and giggled.

"Ah, modern youth has come out to watch an old-fashioned play!"

They hadn't noticed the middle-aged man and the woman approaching until they were beside them.

Sun Wangquan shrugged Qiaoying aside, and bobbed his head in greeting.

"I don't remember seeing an application for permission," Ma Zhiguo, secretary of the commune went on in a needling voice. "But this is what they call freedom of choice."

"Actually . . . we were school friends. . . " Sun Wangquan stammered.

The woman, Supervisor Zhang of the Women's League, covered her mouth and giggled.

"Secretary Ma, the connection was made at school. How sweet!" she gushed, "Wangquan is twenty-one and Qiaoying must be nineteen."

It was not what she said but her tone which annoyed Qiaoying.

"What if the connection was made in school?" she retorted. "We grew up together and we went to school together. The rest came naturally. It's not against the law."

"Of course it's not against the law," said Ma Zhiguo rubbing his paunch complacently.

"We were just conducting a little survey, and so far we've counted, oh, forty-seven couples. These are young people that the law wishes to protect and provide for. We're going to put in a report, and request funds to build a community center, so you will have a place to go relax, to take courses . . . or see each other."

"That's what they said after the fall of the Gang of Four. But that was four years ago," mumbled Qiaoying.

"Everything takes time. I should like to have the Youth League's opinion," Ma Zhiguo said. He clapped Wangquan across the shoulder and moved on.

The woman lingered a moment. She picked off a leaf that had fallen on Qiaoying's shoulder.

"In the year you've been back, you've achieved a lot. People admire you for introducing scientific farming methods, but they still talk behind your back."

"What are they saying?"

"It's just the way you look. You ought to pay more attention to your clothes."

"But I do. This is the way the new socialist farmer should look!"

"Stubborn thing." Her tone didn't show whether or not the Supervisor of the Women's League was angry. "Look at those shoes with the half heels, and those form-fitting slacks. What sort of outfit is that for a farmer? Now look at Wangquan. He's as solid as a brick. He's a farmer and he looks like a farmer!" She gave Qiaoying's shoulder a gentle tap.

"Does being a farmer mean I have to walk around in rags?" Qiaoying was angry now. "If they can wear these clothes in the city, I can wear them here. People called me cheap because I wore sandals. Now you're wearing them too. Somebody had to take the lead."

"I was only trying to be kind," the woman whined. "Secretary Ma, did I say something wrong?"

The man pursed his lips.

"It's not what you wear, it's the motive behind it that matters," he said at length.

"I was told that one time you drove a donkey carrying manure down to the fields. You were reading all the way. In fact you were so wrapped up in reading you drove the donkey back without unloading the manure. Was that true?"

"Who said that?" Qiaoying's face clouded.

"I'm also told you two are studying for another try at the university entrance exams. You want to get out that badly?"

"I . . . I . . . " Sun Wangquan started to say something. Qiaoying gave him a pinch and cut him short.

"Actually we have been studying together. Is it against the rules?"

"I didn't say it wasn't allowed. The country needs educated men and women. But I'm thinking about our village. You young people go off to university, or you join the army. Once you go, you don't come back. Who is going to take on the task of modernizing this district? The most pressing problem in these Taihang Mountains is water for man and beast. A thousand years of the old society did nothing to solve the problem. Today, thirty years after the revolution, the problem is still with us.

"What are we going to do? Our young women want to leave these mountains. And young women from the outside won't come here. There are too many men without women. One day the village will die out. I don't see this as an ideological problem. I see it as a practical one." He dropped his bantering tone, and continued solemnly, "You both graduated from a high school in the city, and you both belong to the Youth League. Wangquan is also the secretary of the branch league. If we can't get help from young people like you, who do we turn to?"

Zhao Qiaoying bit her lip. There was nothing she could say in reply. As soon as the pair was out of earshot, she wheeled on Wangquan.

"You're a fine one," she flared, "letting them talk to me like that.

At least you could have stuck up for me!"

"I did try," he protested, "but your clothes are too western, and you don't take your work seriously. That day when I was carrying a slab of rock down the mountain ... "

She did not let him finish.

"I don't have to listen to this!" Her anger spilled over. "Since I don't suit you, why don't you go build the pig's trough for Duan Xifeng, and marry into her family while you're at it!"

"How did you know?" he asked, astonished.

"News travels fast in this speck of a village," she said bitterly. "Are you going to tell me about it?"

The evening was spoiled.

* * *

Sun Wangquan went up the mountain at dawn that morning. At midday he carried down a stone slab, and while he was having his meal his father told him to go to Duan Xifeng's house and help with a bit of masonry.

"I'll go tomorrow," said Wangquan. "My tools are on the mountain."

"Use mine," his father would not be put off. "I want you to go today. Your Third Auntie will be there too."

The job was to finish a stone pig trough which Duan Xifeng's husband was building before he died two years ago. Duan Xifeng brought tea and cigarettes and put them beside him as he worked. The Third Auntie hung about watching him. Duan Xifeng flitted in and out of the house, urging him not to overexert himself. After a while the Third Auntie insisted that he rest awhile inside. He allowed himself to be dragged into the house. No sooner had he sat on the kang when Duan Xifeng appeared with her quick, light steps, and placed a bowl of scrambled eggs in front of him.

"Oh, my," exclaimed the old woman, "doesn't that look good! But aren't you forgetting someone?"

Xifeng blushed.

"Mother is expecting you in her room," she said.

Xifeng was wearing a new suit of clothes. She hovered over Wangquan as he ate, racking her brain to make conversation.

"It's just a little snack. I'll start supper soon, and after supper we'll go and watch the play. The trough doesn't have to be finished right away. Everybody's going to the fair. It'll be quite something. You're left-handed just like Xiuxiu's father . . . the way you work . . . and the way you hold your cigarette reminds me of him . . . "

How could I remind her of Laifu, Wangquan wondered. He said aloud, "I heard about Laifu's accident. I was away at school then. Was he working on a well?"

Laifu had been digging a well in the canyon. There was a huge rock that had to be blasted at the bottom of the shaft. Laifu went down and lit the charge. But the rope on the hoist slipped its winch.

"By the time they got the rope back on, it was too late."

Xifeng's eyes brimmed with tears that rolled down her cheeks. Wangquan noticed her child, Xiuxiu, had come into the room while they were talking, and was playing on the floor. The toddler was also dressed in new clothes. The child looked up at its mother, wondering what might be wrong. Xifeng wiped away her tears and forced a smile.

"Let's not talk about sad things," she said. She picked up the child and went into the inner room. In a moment she was back with a handful of money which she carefully laid in front of Wangquan.

"Get some decent clothes."

"What's this for?" Wangquan was astonished.

The young woman bowed her head and blushed.

"It's the custom," she finally squeezed out in a small voice, and hurried into the other room.

Xifeng's mother came in then, wreathed in smiles. She lit a cigarette for Wangquan and settled down beside him prattling happily, complimenting him on his work.

"What a joy! Xifeng and I will have someone to depend on again," she said.

Wangquan finally got the drift of what was going on.

"Auntie, about the money," he started to say.

"A gift of clothing is the custom, after things are settled between a couple. My Xifeng says you are an educated man, and you'd probably want to buy them yourself. My daughter's had many prospects since my son-in-law died, but she didn't care for any of them. She wants you. I hope this bit of money will do."

"You mean, you want me for a son-in-law?" Everything had become quite clear to Wangquan now.

"Didn't your father tell you?" Xifeng's mother rose and went into the inner room. The Third Auntie came in almost immediately. She settled herself on the kang unceremoniously and launched into the history of the Duan family. It occurred to Wangquan then that the Third Auntie was not only a gossip, but a tireless matchmaker.

The Duan family were refugees from Hebei, who had settled in the village several generations after the Sun family founded it. Whereas the Sun family had multiplied, the Duans did not. Perhaps a curse had been laid upon them. Xifeng's grandfather had only one son. He, in turn, had only one daughter. To keep the Duan line alive, a son-in-law was brought into the family for Xifeng. He fathered a girl and went to an early grave. Xifeng's father died of a broken heart shortly afterwards. Xifeng's mother vowed on his deathbed that she would bring another son-in-law into the house to produce a male to carry on the Duan line.

"They don't mind you being poor. In time everything will be yours."

The Third Auntie lit a fresh cigarette, and went on. "Xifeng is clever and pretty. And she's a woman. She knows how to make a man happy. So she's three years older than you. But an older woman knows things. You'll see, by and by. Well, Wangquan what do you say?"

Wangquan wanted to get up and run. But Xifeng's shadow on the curtain covering the doorway between the two rooms made him stop.

"I'll think about it," he said.

"That's the spirit!" crowed the Third Auntie, hammering her leg that had gone to sleep. "The dowry hasn't been settled yet. These people are prepared to be generous, but you mustn't be greedy either. They'll be good to you."

The curtain parted and Xifeng came in blushing.

"Leave Xiuxiu with your mother tonight, and go watch the play. Poor Xifeng, you've had a hard time without a man about the house. And you so young to be widowed!"

The Third Auntie glanced sharply from her to Wangquan,

"Of course, I'll go to the play," said Xifeng, with a catch in her voice.

* * *

"Well, go on. Your Xifeng is right over there, by the grave mound," Qiaoying gave Sun Wangquan a shove.

The young woman standing by the grave mound was not interested in the play. She kept turning her head and peering into the shadows under the scholar tree.

Qiaoying drew Wangquan into her arms again and held him tightly.

"Don't think you can get away that easily," she said. "I passed her house this afternoon, and I recognized the sound of you pounding stone. I stood outside the gate while you were sitting on the young widow's kang eating scrambled eggs, having a good time. It drove me wild." She nestled against him.

Wangquan tried to laugh it off. "I didn't accept," he said.

"But you didn't refuse either!"

"I couldn't do that without hurting her feelings. Besides, you've had your prospects too."

"So what? You avoided me for almost a year. How long is a woman supposed to wait for you to ask?"

"How can I ask, when I know that all you want is to get out of these mountains."

"Why can't we go together."

Wangquan's arms went around her. "You think I haven't thought of that? But I thought you wanted someone from the city."

"If I was willing to sell myself, I'd have married long ago. But I want you . . . only you . . . " She lifted her face to his. "Don't sell yourself to the Duans. You're not a baby-making machine. You're a man. Let's really study together and try for the university entrance exams again. Even if we fail, there's still a chance for job assignments outside. All we have to do is make up our minds."

Wangquan brushed the fallen leaves from Qiaoying's hair and stroked her cheek. The blood pounding through his head drowned out the rest of her words. He saw in her eyes a dawn of new hope in life. He could fight her no more. He drew her to him, and led her toward the empty fields.

The young woman beside the grave mound did not move. She watched them disappear into the outer darkness, and began to cry quietly.

Chapter 3

After a heavy rainfall the streams of the Taihang Mountains were again rushing and babbling towards the lowlands. The Qinglong River shook off its lethargy and took on a new vitality. As it wound its way down through the mountains, passing groves of flowering scholar trees, it gathered up strings of blossoms and fallen petals which danced on the currents. Somewhere to the east of Old Well Village the river suddenly vanished into the earth, leaving its cargo of flowers to wither and rot on the pebbles of the dry river bed. Just as mysteriously as it disappeared, the Qinglong River bubbled forth again, two miles west of the village, flowing westward. The water is cool and clear. But it is a placid river now, its boisterousness a memory. Life is sometimes like that.

* * *

Before Sun Wangquan and Zhao Qiaoying had ever appeared in public together, the three families, Sun, Zhao and Duan were embroiled in disputes.

Wangquan's grandfather, Sun Wanshui, had schemed and plotted his grandson's marriage for some time. The great stumblingblock was always poverty, so the Duan family's proposal came as an answer to all his prayers. Because his grandson would be marrying into the Duan family, it would cost the Suns nothing. On the contrary, it would bring in a handsome marriage settlement to be put aside for the day when Wangquan's younger brother would look for a wife. It was a brilliant coup which the old man was determined to carry out. He would brook no opposition from Wangquan. He stood in his courtyard and raged at his grandson, demanding that he marry Duan Xifeng.

With Wangquan's father he adopted a softer tone.

"Qiaoying is not the kind that will settle down," he wheezed. "One of these days, a worker from the city will come along, and she'll run off with him."

"But the girl is his choice," the father tried to reason with the old man.

Sun Wanshui pondered that for a moment.

"I suppose we could consider it, if the Zhaos don't demand too much in the way of a marriage settlement. Then a couple of babies might slow her down . . . "

Somehow Qiaoying's father got wind of this conversation and flew into a rage.

"So, another person's daughter is a lump of gold, and mine is horse dung," he snorted. "We'll see about that. Her food allowance is fifty yuan a year. That makes a thousand yuan in twenty years. Give me a thousand yuan and they can take her. Now if it was a good family, I might reconsider. But what has Wangquan got to offer? He can wrap himself in eighteen quilts and dream! As for you, Qiaoying, if you have a thousand yuan to give me, you can do as you please. Otherwise, you can save your breath!"

Meanwhile, Xifeng's mother enlisted the services of Third Auntie as go-between. The old busybody scuttled tirelessly between the two households bearing gifts. One day it would be a carton of good cigarettes for Wangquan's father; the next day it would be a box of biscuits from the city for Sun Wanshui. Although a man who married into a woman's family was no longer required to make a humiliating public declaration that he was assuming her family name because of his worthlessness, taking her name was still considered shameful. Few men would agree to such a wedding in their own village, particularly if the prospective groom were an educated man.

Xifeng and her mother were keenly aware of these obstacles,

which they spared no expense to overcome. In their determination to snare Wangquan they would even overlook his liaison with Qiaoying.

The village buzzed with gossip. While their elders were trying to strike a marriage bargain, the young couple slipped out at night to meet on the river bank, carried away with love and desire, joy and pain, hope and despair. The elders went about their business as though the lives of these two young lovers had nothing whatever to do with them. Except for a few friends of their own age who stood by them, the village had turned its back on Wangquan and Qiaoying.

Ironically, just then Qiaoying's father received a registered letter summoning him back to the tool factory that had laid him off in '62. As soon as he left for the city, tongues began to wag. It was generally supposed that Qiaoying would soon follow her father. It was then that Wangquan and Qiaoying realized that no one took their relationship seriously. Their ancestors married according to the command of their parents, and arrangements were made through matchmakers. That was the way it was.

Time was running out for the lovers. Wangquan and Qiaoying decided to marry the next day. Sun Wangcai, Egg Head, volunteered to steal a letter of introduction for a marriage certificate from his father. But the plan went awry. When Sun Wanshui heard of it, he locked Wangquan in the house. Qiaoying helped him escape through a window at the back, but before they could get away, Sun Wanshui appeared.

"Wangquan, stay where you are!" shouted the old man, brandishing a sod chopper.

He shrugged off his tunic and stood there trembling.

"You'll have to leave over my dead body!" Sun Wanshui raised the sod chopper ominously. Knowing the old man's violent nature no one dared intervene. Wangquan's gaze went from the desperate face of the old man to the knife gleaming in his hand. He knew this was not an empty gesture. Sun Wanshui was as good as his word. Something cold and implacable gripped Wangquan's heart. It was the death of hope.

* * *

The fierce old man, Sun Wanshui, had become a legend in his own time.

In the twenty-fourth year of the Republic there was a great drought. Day after day the sun blazed down, and the earth hardened and cracked. The people of Old Well Village prayed for rain. Ordinarily the statue of the Dragon King would be taken out of the temple and carried in solemn procession through the village. But the drought was particularly severe that year, and the people needed a miracle. It was said that the Dragon King who presided over the Sun family's native village two hundred miles away had answered many prayers, so a plot was hatched to abduct him and bring him to Old Well Village. Villages sometimes shared the protection of a Dragon King whose favors were jealously guarded. The Dragon King could not be borrowed, but in Shanxi and Hebei provinces there was a tradition of abducting him in times of need. Although he was taken by stealth, he must be returned with honor, especially if he answered the prayers of his abductors. The Dragon King would be decked out in a new robe and carried home in a sedan chair, accompanied by fifes and drums and firecrackers.

The abduction had to be carried out by a strong and virtuous youth, and the lot fell to Sun Wanshui, the oldest son of Sun the Mason.

Sun Wanshui set out for his native village, and within a day and a night returned with the clay figure of the Black Dragon King splendidly decorated with gold paint. Sun Wanshui had been attacked by wild dogs on his way home. Although he was severely mauled, he managed to protect the Black Dragon King, who remained unscathed. The village elders were greatly relieved. Surely such piety would not go unrewarded.

After prayers and incense were offered, the Black Dragon King was paraded through the village with great pomp and circumstance, that he might witness the suffering of the people. Then he was installed in the temple. Thirty virgin youths who were shut in the temple took turns offering prayers and incense day and night. The youths fasted and prayed seven days and nights, but the Black Dragon King was unmoved. The skies continued to blaze. There was no rain in sight. The Ceremony of Incense had failed. The worried elders murmured among themselves that something must have displeased the Black Dragon King. Perhaps it was some secret sin of the principal celebrant that offended the deity. That person was Sun the Mason, who came of a good family, and was considered an honorable and pious man. Sun the Mason himself was perplexed at the failure, for which he felt a personal responsibility. He pondered the problem carefully. It seemed that the ceremony of atonement was necessary to placate the god. This was a ritual performed only as a last resort. The elders were not eager to agree to such a plan because the ritual required a penitent who would take on the sins of the village, and by his suffering pacify the god. The three sons of Sun the Mason were quick to volunteer.

"This requires the toughened body of a mature man," countered Sun the Mason. He had already made up his mind to undertake the ordeal himself. While his sons honed the knives for the ceremony, Sun the Mason prayed before the ancestral shrine, then locked himself in his room with a jug of wine.

Next morning the village crackled with excitement. A throng gathered in front of the Dragon King's temple, wondering breathlessly who the penitent would be.

Shortly after midday, men with bells tied to their waists, marched along brandishing horsetail switches to clear a path through the crowd. Then came drums and gongs setting up an ear splitting clamor. Men carrying huge firecrackers were next. The firecrackers were lit and held in their hands. Each firecracker exploded with three loud blasts, spewing clouds of acrid smoke into the air. A small sedan chair carrying the Black Dragon King moved slowly out of the temple, followed by the Red, White, Yellow and Purple Dragons. Behind the procession of Dragons came blood offerings fastened to a small portable altar. There were fish and cakes; a live goat that rolled its eyes in fright, and a pig that squealed miserably. The appearance of the blood offerings heightened the excitement of the crowd.

Finally the penitent emerged from the gloom of the temple.

Sun the Mason was stripped to a loin cloth. Around his neck was a collar made of three sod choppers fastened in the shape of a triangle with their blades turned inward. Where the three knives met, three more blades were fixed also in a triangle whose apex was at the top of the penitent's head. Sun the Mason's arms were rigidly out-stretched. A hook was passed through the flesh under each arm just above the elbow, to which two more blades were attached.

A great cry went up from the crowd. Never before had they been confronted with such a spectacle. Sun the Mason moved forward slowly. With each step the knives dug into his flesh. Soon his head and shoulders were covered with wounds, and the flesh began to tear under his arms. As he passed, people prostrated themselves, wailing to the heavens. The clash of drums and gongs, the wailing, the broiling heat of the sun, the stench of blood and sweat, the searing pain blended and separated. Sun the Mason stumbled on in a trance, a smile congealed on his face. A man followed him with a kettle of water, dousing the penitent from time to time to drive off the swarms of flies that settled on the torn flesh.

And so the procession crept towards Red Dragon Grotto on top Red Dragon Hill. Red Dragon Hill was the only corner of the mountains that had escaped the woodsman's ax. Once a stele had stood before the temple which read: "He who cuts my trees shall reap my vengeance." Though the temple was in ruins, and the stele had disappeared, the dire warning still hung over the place.

The procession stopped when it reached the temple. Sun the Mason was helped into the main hall, and the knives he wore were removed to let him rest. He lay on the flagstones barely conscious. His followers begged him to turn back, but he did not seem to hear. His eyes were fixed on a faded mural. As he gazed upward the light rekindled in his glazed eyes. The figures on the wall leaped out at him. The red-faced Dragon King in rich court robes sat astride a huge rampant dragon from whose gaping maw a stream flowed from the heavens to the earth below. A host of lesser dragons, gods and demons surrounded him. There was the God of Thunder with a bird-like head, beating his drums, and an old crone, the Lady of Lightning, juggling her darts. The mural wavered before his eyes. The figures beckoned to him, and he knew his ordeal was not over.

Sun the Mason struggled to his feet, and asked that the knives be refastened. Though his followers protested, he would not be denied.

"I must reach Red Dragon Grotto," he said, giving them his fixed, benign smile.

So the painful pilgrimage resumed. Sun the Mason could no longer hold up his arms. He shuffled along, propelled by an immovable faith.

"Dragon King . . . forgive . . . forgive . . . forgive . . . " he pleaded deliriously, leaving a trail of blood in the dust. Somehow Sun the Mason reached Red Dragon Grotto.

The following day he was carried home, dead.

Wanshui, who had been mauled by the wild dogs, was home nursing an infected leg that had swollen to twice its normal size. When he heard the commotion outside, he tumbled off the kang, and limped out to see what had happened. At the sight of his two brothers weeping over their father's corpse, he flew into a rage.

He seized the two young men by the scruff of the neck and shook them.

"Stop snivelling," he commanded, "and help me take down the door."

The two startled brothers hastened to comply. When the door was taken down, Wanshui leaned against it and ordered his brothers to carry him to the Temple. He stumbled into the main hall where the Dragon King sat. He untied the rope used to fasten the sedan chair to its carrying poles, and in a minute had trussed up the Dragon King. He dragged the statue out of the hall, threw the end of the rope over a beam, and shouted for his brothers to hoist it up.

"We'll broil him in the sun!" cried Wanshui.

"That's sacrilege," protested Wanshan.

Wanshui knocked him to the ground with a hard fist to the mouth. The other brother, Wanjin, more strong-willed, took hold of the rope and hoisted the Black Dragon King into the air. There it dangled, under the scorching sun. The villagers were aghast. A few brave souls begged Wanshui to take down the Black Dragon King, fearing eternal damnation. But Wanshui was adamant.

"If we are damned it will be on my head," he snorted.

Armed with sod choppers, the three brothers guarded the Black Dragon King. The crowd now stood back and watched fearfully. A few of the youths who had fasted and prayed jeered at the desecrated deity. Others ran home, terrified that the god's vengeance would surely overtake them.

The Dragon King was powerless now as he slowly turned at the end of his rope under the hot sun. Perhaps it was a trick of the light, but the great horned head with its bulging eyes, flared nostrils, and wide open jaws had lost its arrogance. It seemed less likely to call down damnation than to plead for rain. For it too was parched.

Clouds began to build on the horizon. Lightning ruffled the lowering sky. A wind rose out of nowhere churning up a great cloud of dust. Then the rain began to fall in drops the size of pennies. Faster and faster it fell until it was a roaring torrent.

Wanshui threw himself down on his knees in the driving rain, lifted his face to the heavens and cried in a loud voice, "Father! I swear by all that is sacred, I will find the source of water!"

Wanshan and Wanjin knelt too. Then the three brothers huddled together and mourned. The storm blew over. The mountainsides were green again. The river was flowing, and in the fields the crops stood tall once more. And the people were content. The blue haze of evening descended on the village, and wrapped it in an embrace of forgiveness and reconciliation.

The people of Niuwang Fort in Hebei did not wait for the Black Dragon King to be returned. A few days later they came and took him back, and Sun Wanshui was fined the price of a satin robe for the deity. When they were gone, San Wanshui destroyed the ancient pot shard that had passed from one generation to the next, and vowed he would never set foot again in Hebei, nor claim kinship with anyone there. Thus, the ancient blood ties with Hebei were severed. The story of how Sun Wanshui subdued the Black Dragon King with a sod chopper passed into legend. Decades later, armed with the same sod chopper, he put an end to the hopes of marriage between Wangquan and Qiaoying.

A few days later it was rumored that Wangquan and Xifeng would be married. Exact details of the settlement were hazy, but it was said the Duan family agreed that Wangquan would retain his family name. However his offspring would bear the name of Duan.

That night Qiaoying slipped quietly out of the village and walked the ten-odd li to town, where she caught a train to the provincial capital. She simply disappeared, and no one heard from her afterward.

People are fickle. Qiaoying's departure swung popular opinion to her side. The Third Auntie, who enjoyed the dubious reputation of being a sorceress, went around claiming that her magic had driven Qiaoying from the village.

The end of the affair gave young people of the village much to think about.

Perhaps life is as unpredictable as the Qinglong River. Happiness comes in a burst, just as the river frolics with strings of scholar tree blossoms. But the brief, gaudy hour quickly fades. It disappears as suddenly and inexplicably as the river sinks into the earth, leaving its playmates to wither and die alone. Happiness passes, but life, like the river, goes on. When the river emerges from the earth again it is clearer, quieter, lonelier. It flows on relentlessly, but it has become a river without joy.

Chapter 4

Wangquan and Xifeng were married as soon as the wheat crop was brought in and the sickles were idle.

On his wedding night, Wangquan drank himself into a stupor. All night Xifeng sat beside him on the kang cleaning up his vomit and making him tea.

Half a month later, Wangquan still slept in his clothes, rolled tightly in his quilt, completely ignoring Xifeng. One night he was wakened by a movement. Xifeng was bent over him, gently unbuttoning his clothes.

"You don't need all this," she whispered, seeing that he as awake. "Undress . . . I'm not a tigress."

Wangquan sat up quickly, shucked off his clothes, wrapped the quilt around himself, settled down again, and lay tensely in the darkness. The minutes dragged on. Each little sound from Xifeng seemed to explode in the dark. Finally she settled down, and the sound of her breathing came soft and even. Then he too fell asleep. At first light Wangquan was wakened again. Something had tickled his arm. Xifeng, clad only in underclothes, was curled up beside him, her pale flesh shimmering in the half light. Her lips moved almost imperceptibly along his arm which stuck out from under his quilt, kissing it again and again. He was fully awake now, but he screwed his eyes shut and tried to be still. Even so she sensed the change in the rhythm of his breathing and knew he was awake. The tears she had been holding back trickled down her cheeks, moistening his arm. Through the quilt that separated them he could feel the silent sobs shaking her. The tear streaked cheek pressed against his arm was cold, and so was the woman shivering beside him. Wangquan turned over, lifted a corner of the quilt and draped it across Xifeng's hips. She snuggled under the quilt, sobbing softly, seeking the warmth of his body. Instinctively he reached a hand around her shoulder, stroking her back in a flood of pity and tenderness. She broke down sobbing. He covered her mouth with his hand, calling her name gently, trying to calm her. She took his hand, pressing it against her lips, covering it with kisses. A hot wave swept through him. Wangquan reached out for her, and Xifeng moved eagerly into the circle of his arms. Her softness pressed tight against his hard body blotted out all his pain and confusion. This is life, he thought dimly, this is life. She stopped crying. She tingled with joy. Her body, so cold a moment ago, was suffused with his heat. All the barriers between them came tumbling down. He pressed into her and she arched herself to receive him. All his anguish faded. A cry of joy ran through his veins ... my woman ... my woman.

Afterwards she nestled against him with a contented sigh. Her fingers gently explored the still unfamiliar terrain of his body. She kissed his mouth, his face. She consumed him with her eyes.

"Xifeng, why are you crying?" It was her mother's voice outside the door.

Xifeng buried her head in the hollow of Wangquan's shoulder.

"Xifeng," there was a note of annoyance in the mother's voice now. "It's time to get up!" She rattled the door-handle.

"Mother!" Xifeng called out, trying to sound angry, but there was an undeniable joy in her voice. Outside there was silence.

Wangquan groped under the pillow for his cigarettes. Xifeng quickly took the match box from him to light it for him. But the box was empty. She tiptoed across the room and found more. She knelt beside him and lit his cigarette. Wangquan lay back watching her every move. The soft, rounded outline of a mature woman's naked body was beautiful in the dawn light. She crept under the quilt again. Her head sought the hollow place in his shoulder. Wangquan lay back smoking. He was discovering little things about the woman beside him. Her face was so close to his that he only saw her large and lustrous eyes, still dewy after the tears, but peaceful too.

* * *

Like the thirsting wild flowers of the mountainside after rain, Xifeng blossomed. Her eyes were no longer filled with a nameless misery. They glowed. She brimmed with vitality. Life was sweet again. She loved. She watched Wangquan's every mood, looking for small ways to please him, catering to all his wants. She was conscious of the differences that separated them: her lack of education, and the fact that the marriage was not his choice. But she was confident too of her love for him, and its power to bind him to her.

For a time, Wangquan found a new anchor in his life. He sought the goodness in the woman he was bound to, and found comfort and love in her body. But the novelty quickly faded. An invisible veil hung between them. A cord stronger than both bound Wangquan to the past, to his lost Qiaoying. Soon he noticed, on certain days of each month, Xifeng and her mother conversing in anxious whispers. Then Qiaoying's angry epithet—"baby-making machine"—would riot through his brain. Those words stuck in him like thorns he could not pull out. With Xifeng, lovemaking was a duty. Although he made all the right moves, for Wangquan it was a meaningless friction of flesh against flesh. It was Qiaoying's unbridled ardor, the passion that plunged him into an abyss like death and raised him up again transfigured, that he longed for.

What was there for the man who had married into the Duan family? Work and more work. The passing days became a blur. Wangquan worked the fields from dawn to dusk. At sundown he would carry home a handful of straw for the pigs or a bundle of twigs for weaving baskets when the evening meal was over. Autumn passed into winter. The fields lay fallow and the days stretched in a monotony of idleness. Wangquan did not touch his books, nor did he take an interest in radio broadcasts. He threw himself on the kang as soon as it was dark, and lay with his eyes shut, brooding. Xifeng was deeply troubled by this change. She did not know what to do. When she found him in a lighter mood she would urge him to go out and see his friends. Wangquan did not resist. After all, a man has to live. He became a night wanderer. As soon as he laid down his bowl after the evening meal, he was out of the house. He would wander across the empty fields and into the woods, or he would visit relatives and neighbors.

One night he wandered down to the banks of the Qinglong River, where the grass was tall. Either instinct or memory had brought him back to the trysting place he once shared with Qiaoying. The bed of reeds they wove was still there, but dry and yellow now. He wrapped his cotton coat around himself against the cold, and lay down on the reeds. A faint, sweetish scent of rotting leaves enveloped him. The wind moaned. He gazed blankly at the sky. The moon, newly risen, was cold and bright . . .

* * *

It was that way a long time ago. The moon was bright and a stiff wind was blowing. Sun Wangquan woke from a fitful sleep, chilled to the bone. He moved closer to the fire which moments before was a crackling blaze, but was now a heap of smoldering embers the wind would tease into flaring up, scattering sparks into the night, and dying down again. His young companions were all asleep. A row of buckets stood lined up all the way to the foot of a low cliff, where a stream trickled down between rocks covered with moss.

Sun Wangquan rubbed the sleep out of his eyes and huddled closer to the fire. They called this stream, one li east of the village, Droplet Spring. Actually it was no more than a thread of water oozing from the rocks, that would take a day and night to fill ten or twenty buckets. The adults could not spare the time to fetch water from Droplet Spring, so the chore was assigned to the youngsters who camped beside it all night while their buckets filled.

A slim young girl of about fifteen suddenly appeared out of the darkness and tiptoed toward the spring. She quietly moved aside the bucket at the head of the line and put down her own in its place.

"Hey!" Wangquan called out to her softly.

She looked around and motioned him to be quiet.

Wangquan picked his way over to her.

"Is your father recovered?" he whispered.

"Not quite," Zhao Qiaoying whispered into his ear. "That's why we're so short of drinking water."

"Wait here. I'll steal some for you."

Wangquan took her bucket and went along the row of buckets that were already filled. He tipped a little from each into Qiaoying's bucket. When the bucket was full, he took Qiaoying by the hand and led her jogging to a small grove of trees. The shadow of the trees hid them. Wangquan wiped the sweat from his brow.

"You better go," he said.

"You're mighty anxious to be rid of me," Qiaoying pouted. Suddenly, she grabbed Wangquan's hand and pushed it into her jacket pocket.

"Something to eat," Wangquan's fingers closed around prunes and dried persimmons. He withdrew his hand and popped a prune in his mouth.

Qiaoying smacked his hand smartly.

"Look at you! a junior high student, and you know nothing about sanitation."

She took the rest of the dried fruits from him, wiping them carefully with her handkerchief before she would let him eat.

"You've been avoiding me at school. Don't you like me anymore?"

"I just stole water for you. Doesn't that prove I like you?"

"Anybody can do that."

She stuffed another prune into his mouth almost violently.

"Sometimes you aggravate me so much—I could bite you!"

Wangquan rolled up his sleeve with a laugh. "All right. Take a chunk of flesh in exchange for the prunes and dried persimmons."

"You call that a fair exchange?"

"Well, what more do you want?" asked Wangquan.

"Come closer . . . I'll whisper in your ear."

Wangquan leaned towards her, and the next moment his ear was clamped between Qiaoying's teeth. Wangquan let out a howl. His hands flew up to push her away, brushing against her budding breasts. That brief contact sent an electric ripple through them. They flew apart.

Qiaoying crossed her arms over her chest, blushing deeply.

"You devil, you devil," she kept muttering.

Wangquan's heart hammered so hard that it made him weak. Sweat beaded his brow.

"You almost bit my ear off," he murmured, dazedly rubbing his ear.

They stood gaping at each other. In that split second something happened, something tender, sweet, intoxicating. In a flash they seemed to have discovered something, and acquired wisdom. But it was too elusive for them to hold on to.

The crickets chirped. The cool wind caressed their faces and hands. The air was filled with magic.

Suddenly their young companions surrounded them shouting and jeering.

"Come on, come on, give us a hug!"

"That wasn't a hug! That was catching a thief!"

"Give us a kiss! Give us a kiss!"

They clapped their hands in rhythm and began to chant: "Qiaoying . . . Wangquan . . . man and wife . . . "

Qiaoying picked up her bucket and stalked away.

"Hey, wait a minute," Egg Head Wangcai went after her. "You can't steal our water and walk away without apologizing!"

Qiaoying wheeled around and threw the bucket of water in Egg Head's face. The water splashed on Wangquan too. It was icy cold.

* * *

Wangquan shook himself. Nothing ever changed. The same moon shone. Memories he could not shake off swirled around him in the night wind and the whispering grass. He leapt to his feet, threw back his head and cried out "Qiaoqiao. Qiaoqia-ooo!" The wind whipped it away, but the echo drifted back to him across the dark void. "Qiaoqiao . . . Qiaoqiao . . . "

I must go on living, he told himself dully. As he walked home in a daze, he met some young men shouting and laughing as they walked to a poker game at Sun Wangcai's. At first Wangquan would not join them. But they kept insisting, so Wangquan finally allowed himself to be dragged along.

Sun Wangquan never went to Egg Head's house. Egg Head's

father was the party secretary and Sun Wangquan was always uncomfortable in his presence. Although they were high school classmates Wangquan and Egg Head did not get along well. Part of the problem was that Wangquan despised Egg Head's obsession with girls. The sight of a pretty girl would turn Egg Head into a mass of quivering jelly, although they treated him with disdain. It was not only his bald and scaly head. That defect he could at least hide under an old army cap. But he also had a rather large, upturned nose with wide flaring nostrils like a stone lion. That unfortunate feature Egg Head could not hide. Some say that the deformed nose was proof positive of congenital venereal disease, a legacy from his father. It was rumored that Egg Head had a certificate from the county hospital declaring that he was disease free, or at least not infectious. But the cynics were quick to point out that these days one could exchange three catties of good sesame oil for any piece of paper one needed. The fact of the matter was that nobody knew the truth about Egg Head's condition. The women avoided him like the plague, though his father was the party secretary, and the family had money and power, a fine house and furniture. They tolerated his crudeness and the occasional pinch and grope, but that is where they drew the line.

Egg Head was also fascinated with women's underclothes, which he stole from laundry lines. He would conceal the stolen bras and panties in his bed, fondling and playing with them. Afterwards he would return them to their owner, by tossing them over the walls of their courtyards, covered in filth. The women were too embarrassed to complain about these antics, but they gossiped among themselves. The more the women shunned Egg Head, the more he desired them. It was rumored that he relieved his lust on dogs and donkeys.

In spite of the ugly stories, Egg Head attracted a group of young hangers-on. His father had built him a house with five rooms and furnished it with everything he wanted. Aside from a chest and a low cupboard, basic furnishings for a rural wedding, there were also items brought in from the city: a tall wardrobe, a chest of drawers, a desk, a sofa and a small side-table. The walls were freshly whitewashed, and decorated with pictures of pretty actresses clipped from film magazines. The new kang was nine feet long. A layer of felt was spread over the mat. On top of the felt was a wool blanket, which was covered in turn by a bedspread. When the electric light was turned on, the room sparkled. Egg Head had everything except a woman.

Sun Wangquan was amazed that such a house existed in a village like Old Well.

"Wangquan! What a surprise!" Egg Head leaped up from the sofa to greet his old classmate. "Have a smoke," he said. "These Phoenixes are rather good."

Wangquan took a cigarette and they lit up. Cigarettes and tea were passed around. Everyone kicked off their shoes and hopped on the kang. Two decks of cards were brought out. Eight people ranged themselves around a low kang table and the game began. Egg Head Sun Wangcai's home was popular with young people because they could do as they pleased without a chaperon. Though Egg Head was crude and a sort of misfit, he had a generous streak. One could always count on him for free tea and cigarettes.

Eight people seated round one small table seemed a bit cramped to Sun Wangquan. But after a few hands he began to grasp the real reason for the crowding. The game was punctuated by giggling and swearing. At first Wangquan thought this was directed at the cards. Then he realized that body leaned against body and furtive hands were at work, pinching, caressing, kneading and exploring. Legs twined. A man's foot glided stealthily along a young woman's thigh.

While the cards were being dealt, a young woman, Chunmei, described a prime time television program she had seen the other day at a guest house in the city.

"They were dancing on ice. The ice was that thick," she indicated the thickness of the ice with her fingers. "The man wore skin-tight pants. The girl's arms and legs were bare. All she had on was a little bit of cloth around her—parts. There they were, holding onto each other, hugging and carrying on with all the lights on, and all those people watching. And then . . . "

She giggled and blushed.

"What happened next?" the others crowed. "What happened next?"

"Then the man spread his legs, and stuffed the girl under them!"

For a moment they looked at each other in disbelief. Then Egg Head's hand came down on the table with a bang.

"Good show!" he shouted. Everybody laughed, shuffling and dealing the cards, studying their hands.

They played the next two hands in silence.

"This is getting boring," a young man called Xizhu said. "Let's do something different."

"We'll play for kisses," Egg Head made a face.

"We'll play for kisses," echoed Xizhu, giving Chunmei a sidelong glance.

"Everybody pick a partner."

"Good," shouted Zhier, who was sitting next to Wangquan. "If we lose, you get to kiss us. That's our tough luck. But what if we win? I don't want to kiss somebody with garlic breath! If we're playing for kisses, I want to be Egg Head's partner!"

"How's that?" Egg Head looked up, his heart skipping a beat, not sure that he heard Zhier correctly.

"Don't get your hopes up, banker," rejoined Zhier. "I chose you because your nose disgusts me."

The sky seemed to crash around Egg Head's ears. He wanted to crawl into the ground.

Chunmei was doubled over with laughter. She threw herself into Xizhu's arms, laughing till the tears rolled down her face. Egg Head did not know whether to laugh or cry. He reached for Zhier's thigh and gave it a hard pinch. Zhier jerked away from him and buried her face against Wangquan's shoulder, laughing and swearing. They rolled on the kang, laughing and shouting in a tangle of arms and legs.

"Kissing is tame," Egg Head said. "These days, strip poker is all the rage in the city!"

"Trust you to think of something like that," Zhier taunted.

"It's true! Our classmate, Fat Wang who works for the county security force told me so. There was a case . . . Every time you lose you have to take off one piece of clothes. When a person is stripped down to the basics, then they strip after every second loss. The game's over when everybody's naked."

"Boys and girls? Together?" Chunmei's eyes were round as saucers.

"Of course," snorted Egg Head, nostrils flaring wider than ever.

They looked at each other, blushing to the roots of their hair.

Just then someone pounded the door, calling for one of the girls. The girls scrambled off the kang, ran their fingers through their hair, slipped into their shoes and left.

"Aren't you going?" Wangquan asked the others as he slid off the kang.

"Have another cigarette," Egg Head urged. "The best part is still to come."

They waited till they heard the gate shut, and the girls' footsteps faded in the distance. Then they struggled into their quilted overcoats, picked up a flashlight and slipped out of the house. The village streets were dark and empty. Wangquan knew instinctively that some mischief was afoot. He wanted to know what they were up to, but Xizhu would only grin mysteriously, and Egg Head beckoned for him to be quiet.

They made their way silently to the miserable little cottage of Wu Erdan nestled in the shadows of Sleeping Tiger Mountain. A light still burned in the window. Wangquan glanced at his watch. It was ten twenty-five. What could they be up to at this hour?

They put out their cigarettes, took off their shoes, brushed aside the prickly vines that covered a gap in the wall and squeezed through. Wangquan did not want to go any further. Egg Head pressed his mouth against his ear and whispered this was a game of detective. Wu Erdan's wife had stolen something, and they were about to get it back for the rightful owner.

"You mustn't make a sound no matter what happens," whispered Egg Head.

Xizhu giggled and Egg Head gave him a kick in the shins.

They slinked across the yard and hid themselves behind a stack of firewood under a shed.

In a moment another figure crept through the gap in the wall. Sun Wangquan poked Egg Head in the ribs, wanting to know who it was. Egg Head responded with a meaningful pinch. The stranger crept stealthily toward the window. He stood peering into the dark, listening. The cottage was silent. He went over to the window, and tapped on the pane. Almost instantly the door opened a crack. The man quickly stepped through it and bolted the door behind him. Wangquan caught a glimpse of the man's face as the door shut. It was the old bachelor Sun Baocheng.

Sun Baocheng was in his late thirties but was too poor to find a wife. He was a lusty man, known to have had affairs with several women, but he had never been linked with the wife of Wu Erdan.

Wu Erdan was a quiet man who never strayed from the side of his wife and child. It was only after the government policy had changed that he had left the village to find work elsewhere. No sooner had he left than his wife had taken up with Sun Baocheng. Suddenly Sun Wangquan was sad and bored. He wanted to leave. He did not want to be in this place with these people. It was quite clear what they were up to now.

Sun Wangquan started to move away. He kicked against a jar in the dark and sent it bouncing across the yard. Instantly the sounds coming from within ceased. Wangcai pinched him to be still. They waited. A while later the sounds of labor resumed. Egg Head and Xizhu moved a ladder and propped it against the window. Egg Head was the first to scramble up the ladder. He slit a hole in the window paper and peered in. Xizhu could not wait his turn. In spite of Egg Head's well aimed kicks to keep him off, he lunged up the ladder too. Sanze, not wanting to be left out climbed up too. It was too much for the rickety ladder. It gave way with a loud crack, and the three young men came tumbling down in a heap. They hurriedly grabbed their shoes and hobbled away.

The light in the cottage snapped off. No one pursued them.

Once they were outside the wall, their panic eased. They struggled into their shoes, cursing and groaning.

Egg Head found a fragment of a brick and lobbed it over the wall. It hit the roof with a crash. "I know who you are!" shouted Egg Head. "I saw what you did! You horny old goat!" Then he let fly a string of obscenities.

Egg Head had twisted his ankle and it began to swell and throb. He limped away supported by Sanze and Xizhu. Still, he managed to belt out a bawdy song in a peculiar falsetto.

Egg Head's song made Wangquan snicker. Then suddenly he wanted to cry, for Egg Head, Sun Wangcai, or for himself. He was not sure which. He had not climbed the ladder, but the sounds he heard did send the blood rushing through him. He longed for Qiaoying—her fiery, urgent love.

As he passed her door, dark and silent now, he wondered where she was. A shadow appeared in front of them. Wangquan stopped.

"Let's go! Why're you looking so stupid, Wangquan?" Xizhu slapped him on the back.

"A fox! It's a fox."

"Where? You must be seeing a ghost." They looked at each other, laughing, and kept on.

Wangquan knew it was a fox. Actually the fox did not run away. Instead, it ran to the front of Qiaoying's house and leaned against the door. It looked back at Wangquan.

"Is that you, Qiaoying?" As Wangquan passed her door, he wondered where she was.

Chapter 5

The passing generations of Old Well systematically denuded the mountains. First the ancient forest was razed. Then the more accessible woods were destroyed. Now the mountainsides were bare. The only legacy the ancients left were the dry shafts of more than ten wells scattered at the foot of Qinglong Mountain and Wohu Mountain. Actually there was a little water in five or six of these wells. But they were unreliable. When the Qinglong River was flowing there was water in the other wells too. But in a drought when the river dried up, the wells failed. For generations the villagers dreamed of sinking a well so deep, that it would tap the underground source of the Qinglong River. Only this way, they thought, could their perennial problem be solved.

In the winter of 1979, the east well, which had been supplying the village, turned muddy. The work brigade decided it was time to dredge, and if possible, to deepen a well. They settled on the west well because it was the deepest, going down about forty-five meters, and was not as old as some of the others. The west well was sunk in the third year of the republic, which made it about the same age as Sun Wanshui. Some of the old-timers still remembered when it was being dug. But it had been allowed to silt up over the years, and gradually became much shallower.

Work began at once.

Before dawn, eight days after they started digging, the crew gathered round a bonfire beside the shaft. It was bitterly cold. There had been a dusting of snow during the night. Wangquan's father, Sun Fugui, the overseer, was having a heated discussion with Sitang, the well expert who had been brought in from Lingdi Village thirty li away to direct the work. Sun Fugui was a taciturn man until he was riled. That morning he was definitely stirred up. While he could not fault Sitang for dredging as fast as he could, he maintained that the shaft was not adequately reinforced. Safety was being neglected. The two men disagreed completely, each sticking to his guns. The argument rose to a fevered pitch. Finally, the two men decided to go down the shaft together to settle the dispute on the spot.

After Sun Fugui and Sitang were lowered into the well, the crew settled around the bonfire again smoking and chatting. They took no notice of a dull rumbling that seemed to come from underground. A louder rumble sent them rushing to the side of the well. The shaft was pitch dark. The lights had gone out. Silence greeted their loud hellos. Something was amiss. The crew threw themselves on the winch. With a loud twang a length of steel cable leaped up and wrapped itself around the crank shaft. The platform to which it was attached had broken loose when the sides of the well collapsed. Wangquan's father and Sitang were buried alive.

By the time Sun Wangquan was summoned from his fields a large crowd was milling around the well. A few well specialists had been hurriedly called in from neighboring villages to direct the rescue operation. There was confusion everywhere. Secretary Ma of the commune, the head of the local clinic, and brigade secretary Sun Fuchang who had also rushed down to the well, stood back from the melee, grimly smoking.

Lights had been strung down the well shaft and a crew was already digging.

Wangquan grabbed hold of one of the well specialists.

"What happened!" he demanded, choking back tears.

"Go home," the man replied. "There's nothing for you here."

He handed Wangquan his cigarette. Wangquan took a few drags and threw it away. Suddenly the sky seemed very bright, and his head felt light. The faces around him were cold, wooden, strange—a nightmare, he thought.

Later the assistant chief of the County work brigade, Zhang Sanhuo arrived. A brief discussion took place between him and the various well experts. The consensus was that there was little hope of finding the men alive.

It was another nine days before the bodies were found. The two men were standing pressed tightly against the sides of the well. When the sides of the shaft first gave way Sun Fugu and Sitang pressed themselves against the sides to avoid the falling rubble. Probably they did not realize the seriousness of their situation until they were pinned against the wall. Sun Fugui clutched Sitang's wrist; and the other held onto his shirt sleeve. This gesture of mutual reassurance became a death grip.

The decaying bodies were wrapped in sacks and brought to the surface. They were laid on mats and sluiced down with water and wrapped in lengths of white cloth so that the crushed bodies had some semblance of human form again. Doctor Ding, chief of the local clinic, who had been a field doctor during the war, supervised the disposal of the bodies.

When the bodies were placed in their coffins the families were allowed to come and claim their dead. The brigade leader from Sitang's village came to claim his body. It was quickly agreed that Old Well Village would provide the shroud, coffin, and transportation to return the dead man to his home. Old Well Village would also pay a compensation of 150 yuan. From that time on, the two villages would have nothing further do to with each other.

Sun Fugui was a widower, and as his sons were grown, the village saw to it that he received a proper burial, and that his aged father Sun Wanshui was provided for. Sun Fugui was a poor and simple man, with nothing to accompany him to the grave except his pipe with a brass bowl and a mouthpiece of white soapstone, and a tobacco pouch embroidered with a pair of mandarin ducks. This symbol of love was stitched by his dead wife when she was still a girl. It was a gift that Sun Fugui treasured all his life, and kept hidden in a box, so it still looked new. These things and two boxes of his favorite biscuits bought from the Supply Depot, were placed in the coffin. A handful of corn husks was set on fire in an earthenware pot, and placed in front of the coffin. At the end, Wangquan's younger brother, Wanglai, placed a heavy bundle in the coffin.

San Wanshui recognized it at once, and the tears poured down his withered old face afresh. His lips trembled so much that it was only with great difficulty that he managed to gasp out: "Enough . . . he's had a tough life . . . surely he doesn't have to cut millstones and dig wells in the next world too . . . "

Wangquan saw that the bundle contained his father's chisel and mallet. He was suddenly filled with loathing. He seized it and hurled it as far as he could. His long, narrow face worked convulsively, and with a loud cry he fell on his knees before the coffin. Wanglai knelt to his left and Xifeng, beside herself with grief, knelt to his right, holding the bewildered child, Xiuxiu.

The men of the village huddled together with their heads bowed; the women cried softly and sobbed. Even the village dogs were quiet, slinking close to the walls.

Someone whispered to Wangquan that it was time to send his father on his way. He rose heavily to his feet, swung his mourning staff high over his head and brought it down with a resounding crack on the earthenware pot before him. The pot shattered instantly, sending up a cloud of ashes and sparks.

"Go," cried the chief mourner in a high singsong voice, and the cortege began to wend its way through the village, across the bridge and into the old graveyard. That day a jeep came out of the city bearing several dignitaries from the county government and floral wreaths. So Sun Fugui was laid to rest with dignity.

Next noon a dedication ceremony was held beside the well at which the villagers reaffirmed their resolution to find water. The first crew to resume work were Sun Wangquan and the Party Secretary Sun Fuchang. Secretary Li of the County Committee had come especially for the occasion, accompanied by a battery of newspaper and radio reporters, and photographers. The Secretary asked concerned questions about safety and posed for photographs with Wangquan and Sun Fuchang, the two men who would direct the work, and on whose shoulders rested the hopes of the entire village.

Duan Xifeng burst into tears when she heard that Wangquan

had taken on the task of dredging the west well.

"It's courting death," she wailed. "Your father has just gone. Xiuxiu's father died digging a well too. If something happens to you, how will we live?"

"You'll go on as before," Wangquan answered dully. "My life isn't more valuable than anyone else's."

Sun Fugui's death was only part of the reason for Wangquan's determination to follow in his father's footsteps. A more pressing reason was locked inside him. The root of his problems was the contradiction of his life with Xifeng. She was the head of the household by day, but when she came to his kang at night her sensuality overwhelmed him. She was a pretty woman. But it was Qiaoying he hungered for. Marriage had become slavery, and lovemaking a task, mechanical, false and joyless. Qiaoying's bitter taunt, "baby-making machine," still festered in his soul. He thought of killing himself but lacked the courage. The well would solve all his problems. One ominous rumble, a moment of terror, then oblivion.

Xifeng did not know all that went on in Wangquan's mind. She thought it was grief that drove her husband. She washed her face carefully and combed her hair, and with eyes red from weeping, went to seek Sun Wanshui's help.

Sun Wanshui squinted at his granddaughter-in-law: "How many in your family died digging wells?" he asked.

"One. Xiuxiu's father."

"I think there were at least three. But our family is old. We've lost at least eight," he made a sign with his fingers. "Let him go, wife of Wangquan. Destiny cannot be changed. If it is his time to die, nothing will save him. But if he does find the source of water, he will bring honor to all those who lie in the old graveyard."

The west well was quickly dredged. Just as they expected, it was over forty-five meters deep, and more than half that depth was chiseled out of solid rock. But they did not find the legendary crevice that leads to the center of the earth. In the eastern corner of the shaft they found what appeared to be a deep hole filled with rocks. Whether this was done deliberately by earlier diggers or was the work of nature, it was hard to tell. However it was obvious that if the well were to be made deeper, they had found the logical starting point. Work continued at a feverish pace.

Day after day, Old Well Village shook as the diggers blasted their way downward. Progress was slower now. Every few days old Sun Wanshui would hobble to the well, leaning on his cane. He had been a stone mason and well digger all his life, and villagers teased him, saying he loved stone more than he loved women. The old man chuckled good humoredly. He'd been quite a lady's man in his youth. His calloused hands were no stranger to female flesh. To him all women were alike. Rock, on the other hand, was fascinating in its endless variety. He knew which types of rock absorbed water and which were impervious. He recognized that layers of stone in certain combinations form a water table. In other combinations water disappeared. Sun Wanshui examined the rocks brought up from the well, and he was certain that they would strike water. But as the diggers went deeper the old man became less certain. He kept his doubts to himself. Wangquan shared his grandfather's fears. The Suns were generations of stone masons and well diggers. Wangquan had apprenticed under his father and knew something about rocks too.

One day Wangquan and Secretary Sun Fuchang went to Sun Wanshui in great excitement, saying that drops of dew were found at the bottom of the well. The old man hobbled down to the well, took a piece of rock that had just been brought up and examined it. The rock was damp, but it was not impervious. The three men went down the shaft to take a closer look. Sun Wanshui drew a gnarled finger across the beaded side of the shaft. If the droplets that appeared again ran together then water was near at hand. If not, it was useless digging any further.

They waited. Droplets of dew popped out on the rock just as the old man said they would, but the droplets were not heavy enough to run together.

Work was stopped at once.

The following day the assistant chief of the county work brigade, Zhang Sanhuo, came to inspect the labor. He did not go down the shaft, but examined a stone that was brought up and pronounced that it was limestone which indicated there was scant hope of finding water. Furthermore the area had been designated as prohibited to well digging for that reason.

Sun Fuchang's face darkened. An ominous silence settled over the assemblage. When he spoke there was anger in Sun Fuchang's voice: "You were here the day the work began. Why didn't you stop us then?"

Zhang Sanhuo's thin lips curled in a sneer: "If I recall correctly, you led the first crew down. And all the higher-ups were egging you on. Who was I to dash cold water on your enthusiasm . . . " He sent the rock rattling to the bottom of the well with a careless flick of the wrist.

Sun Fuchang flushed a deep purple.

As Zhang Sanhuo turned away, Sun Wangquan confronted him.

"You're putting us under a death sentence," he blurted out.

"Not exactly," Zhang Sanhuo said pleasantly. "The prohibition was put in place because we lack technology to locate the water table in this terrain. And we lack the means of sinking deep wells, but things change."

"Then the prohibition is temporary," persisted Wangquan.

But Zhang Sanhuo did not seem to hear.

"How deep have you gone?" he asked.

"About eighty-six meters." Tears came to Wangquan's eyes. His father's death, the failure to reach water in the west well, and now the prohibition. It was too much to bear. The rebellious blood of the Suns that flowed in Wangquan's veins would give him no peace. A few days later he gathered together his friends Xizhu, Egg Head, Sanze and several other young men and presented a plan to dredge the Twin Wells.

"But the Twin Wells belong to Stone Gate Village," objected Xizhu.

"Not so," countered Wangquan. "The well to the east might be theirs. But the one closest to us definitely belongs to Old Well Village. There's a stone tablet at the bottom that proves it."

The Twin Wells were an east and west cistern three meters apart. They were two li from Old Well Village but only half a li from Stone Gate Village. So they technically belonged to the latter. However, a man named Huang who owned the land around the wells bequeathed them to Old Well Village when he went to live there. The Huang family died out a few generations earlier, and ownership of the wells reverted to Stone Gate Village. The people of Old Well Village stopped fetching water from Twin Wells.

Gradually the wells filled with silt. The wells were abandoned then, and no one went near them afterward.

The existence of a stone tablet recording the rightful ownership of the well galvanized the group of young men into action. Armed with old buckets and basins they stole out of the village in the dead of night and began dredging the well to the west. They were swept along on a wave of euphoria, no obstacle could hinder them. The well was dredged in no time, and the water was clear and sweet again. To crown their achievement, they found a stone tablet set above the water line recording the history and ownership of the well.

The young men were elated. The well was theirs and they worked at it till dawn when the first villagers from Stone Gate arrived with their buckets. There was an argument at first, but when a stone tablet was mentioned, the villagers retreated. A while later the secretary of the village appeared. He read Wangquan's copy of the inscription on the stone tablet several times and went away without a word, his brow knit in a deep frown. The young men let out a whoop of joy and raced back to their homes. The news quickly spread through Old Well Village. As soon as the morning meal was over people streamed to the western twin well, some carrying buckets, and others going down for a glimpse of the stone tablet. A crowd from Stone Gate Village surrounded the well in the meantime, and were busily shoveling earth into it.

Wangquan and his friends tried to stop them. The Secretary who was directing the work smiled coolly at him. "I was hoping you'd come back. I want to know where that inscription came from. There is a tablet in the well all right, but the inscription is all worn out and undecipherable."

Wangquan was speechless with rage. He clambered down the well. When he came up again he was covered with mud from head to toe. He seized the Secretary of Stone Gate Village by the collar and shook him.

Sun Fuchang, the Secretary of Old Well Village, who was on the scene, separated them. "If you have something to say, Wangquan, say it quietly," Sun Fuchang said mildly.

"They've destroyed the inscription on the tablet!" Wangquan spat out angrily.

Sun Fuchang turned to the Secretary of Stone Gate Village grimly. "What you've done today is criminal. I think you might have some difficulty explaining it away."

"Explain what?" shouted the Secretary of Stone Gate Village. "You claim the well belongs to your village. Prove it. If you can't, then you're trespassing!" He looked around at the men armed with picks and shovels. "Fill it!"

"Not so fast!" Sun Wanshui pushed through the crowd, and faced the Secretary of Stone Gate. "Scoundrel!" he spat at the Secretary, his straggly beard quivering. "Scoundrel! So you will play the bully."

The men of Stone Gate Village recognized the fierce old man and dropped their tools in spite of themselves. Also they were outnumbered if it came to a fight.

"I know of a tablet." The Third Auntie came hobbling out of the crowd. To Sun Fuchang and Sun Wanshui she said: "My man said according to the inscription on the tablet, Old Well Village paid taxes on the three-quarter mu of land surrounding the twin wells. If the land was ours, then the wells are ours too."

"Where is the tablet?" Sun Fuchang wanted to know.

"Well, it was originally in front of the Guanyin Temple."

"But where is it now?" cried Sun Fuchang impatiently.

"Right now ... " The Third Auntie's voice sank to a whisper. "We're using it as the floor of our latrine."

Laughter rippled through the crowd but the mood did not lighten.

Sun Wanshui beckoned Wangquan to his side: "Take a look at it. If it's any use, bring it."

Wangquan and his friends raced off to their village.

The Secretary of Stone Gate Village cast a meaningful glance at his men, and several quietly melted from the crowd.

By the time Wangquan and his friends were back, the villagers from Stone Gate had surrounded the well, armed to the teeth.

Wangquan planted the tablet on the ground and shouted, "Carved in the seventh year of Tongzhi! Read it!"

"Read a stinking latrine board?" The men around the well hooted with laughter, brandishing their weapons.

"Fill the well!" shouted the Secretary of Stone Gate Village.

The die was cast. The men put their shoulders to the task.

Sun Wanshui hefted a carrying pole. "There hasn't been a fight in twenty years," he muttered. "May the gods have mercy on me." He charged the men of Stone Gate Village. The people of Old Well Village followed him into the fray. The fight was quickly over. Carrying poles were no match for picks and shovels. The villagers from Old Well were routed. The men of Stone Gate did not press their advantage, but turned again to the task of filling the well as quickly as they could.

They did not notice Sun Wangquan dashing toward them until he was almost upon them. Still they did not take heed for Wangquan was empty-handed, nor did they realize his intent until he plunged into the cistern. A dull thud came from the well, then there was silence. Duan Xifeng who had come from the village just then let out a wild scream, and the villagers from Old Well stormed the well.

The men of Stone Gate dropped their tools and ran.

Late in the day the Secretary of the Commune, the County Secretary of the Party, and the Chief of Security descended upon the village. An investigation was hurriedly completed, and the dispute was settled. Those injured in the fighting were made personally responsible for their medical expenses. The Secretary of Stone Gate Village was found guilty of inciting violence and stripped of his party membership. The Secretary of Old Well Village got off with a stiff reprimand for leaving the scene of disturbance, and for not attempting to stop the fight. On the basis of the inscription on the stone tablet found in the Third Auntie's latrine, and Sun Wangquan's copy of the text on the tablet in the well, the dispute was settled in favor of Old Well Village.

The downfall of the arrogant Secretary of Stone Gate Village and the acquisition of a usable well was cause for celebration. Sun Wanshui dressed the wounds on his grandson's leg and set a small table in his courtyard with plates of dried beancurd, strips of yam, cabbage and peas and a jug of wine. The two sat drinking and talking. The old man's eyes gleamed with excitement and pride. He wanted to know everything about the well, and Wangquan happily obliged.

"Tonight we're going to get drunk," the old man crowed. He topped his cup and tossed it down. The wine burned all the way down his gullet. His brain was beginning to fog. He shook his head to clear it. The lines of a riddle floated, unbidden to the surface of his mind.

"There's an old riddle," Sun Wanshui muttered, and he started to recite: *When the stone dragon comes alive, rain will fall.* No one knew the meaning of that riddle until one of our ancestors by the name of Sun Xiaolong unraveled it."

The story of Sun Xiaolong was a family legend that Wangquan had heard many times. Sun Xiaolong, whose name means "Little Dragon," was an exceptionally talented stone carver. He was obsessed with the idea of solving the riddle, and roamed the mountains in quest of the stone dragon. One day he found a rock in a cave which glowed red and purple in the dark. Sun Xiaolong carved a dragon on that rock. Although it glowed with incandescent fire it was not alive. In his frustration Sun Xiaolong struck the stone dragon with his fist and cut his hand. A drop of blood was smeared on the dragon, and the creature began to twitch. Sun Xiaolong quivered with excitement. He pricked his finger and ran it along the outlines of the dragon. The beast writhed, but the stone held it captive. Only blood could set it free. Sun Xiaolong found a lamb which he killed and he smeared the stone dragon with its blood. "It didn't work," mused the old man. "It wanted Sun Xiaolong's blood. And Xiaolong stabbed himself with his chisel and his blood released the stone dragon ... "

"Not so, Grandfather," Wangquan cut across Sun Wanshui's story. "Sun Xiaolong tore his heart out with his bare hands, and the blood spewed all over the rock. That's what released the dragon. It's the same Taihua Red Dragon we worship in the Dragon King Temple."

Sun Wanshui's eyes snapped wide. "How would you know?" he demanded.

Sun Wangquan shook his head, trying to concentrate. He too was drunk.

"I think I've always known," he said finally. "The night my father died, I dreamed I was Xiaolong ... and that I plucked my heart out with my bare hands ... I woke Xifeng with my scream." He gave an embarrassed giggle. "The birthmark on my chest has ached ever since."

Sun Wanshui gazed at his grandson dully. He raised a trembling finger and rested it gingerly on his grandson's chest.

"Let me see."

Sun Wangquan undid his shirt. Between his hard pectorals was an angry red birthmark. The birthmark had troubled the elders of the village when he was born, for it resembled a jagged wound. But in time, it was forgotten.

"Xiaolong."

"What's the matter, Grandfather?"

"Nothing." Sun Wanshui was deep in thought.

"There have only been two exceptional men in this family since our ancestor left Hebei a thousand years ago," Sun Wanshui said: "The pioneer Sun Laoer and Sun Xiaolong. Perhaps you will be the next one. You're educated, and your horizons are broad. If you find the source of water, this village will stand forever."

He poured another cup of wine, and lumbering to his feet, offered it to Wangquan. "I offer you this cup, Grandson. Drink!"

Wangquan poured a cup and offered it to the old man. "You must drink too, Grandfather!"

The two men raised their cups.

The peaks of the Qinglong Mountains reared against the night sky. The moon, new-risen, flooded the courtyard with shimmering light. Wangquan lifted his face to the sky and made a silent vow to find water for Old Well Village or die trying. Sun Wanshui swayed on his feet and moved unsteadily towards his room. On the doorstep he paused and spoke in a croaky voice: "I know life is hard with the Duans . . . I know you still want Qiaoying . . . and you want to leave. I should not have interfered. But it's done. Find us water, Wangquan. Then, if you still want to leave and find Qiaoying, I won't stand in your way." He lapsed into silence.

The untimely death of his son; the fight between the villages; Wangquan's headlong plunge into the well and the legend of Sun Xiaolong whirled through his brain. Suddenly he was choked with tears. He stumbled across the threshold and shut the door. Wangquan watched his grandfather go. His heart seized up into a cold, hard lump. He was numb. It's too late, he thought to himself. Qiaoying is gone.

The night sky arched over him, dark and empty.

Chapter 6

The jeep bounced along the mountain road, passed the old grave yard, then sped down a long slope to Old Well Village. Branch Secretary Sun Fuchang and Sun Wangquan who were sitting on the stone railing of the bridge waiting, rushed forward as soon as the jeep came to a stop.

Three men got off and stood in a cloud of exhaust fumes shaking hands all around and exchanging pleasantries. The three were engineer Wang of the Water Resources Office, Zhang Sanhuo of the county brigade in charge of well construction, and a white-haired intellectual. Engineer Wang, who was making the introductions in his usually hearty fashion, pointed out that Geologist Sun's forebears came from the region.

Sun Fuchang clasped the geologist's hand in both of his, "We are honored to have someone so distinguished take an interest in our poor village."

"It is I who am honored," the geologist smiled shyly. He was a thin old man, who resembled a bundle of twigs wrapped in parchment. "Whether we find water depends on nature. We will see . . . " His eyes lit on Wangquan, and his face crinkled into a smile. "Ah, there you are, the young man with the lock." Wangquan smiled too.

They had met earlier that day. Sun Fuchang, his son Egg Head and Sun Wangquan had taken a tractor and gone into town at the crack of dawn. Egg Head was hoping to find work in the town, and perhaps a wife too. Wangquan wanted to escape the home and the role of "baby-making machine." The death of his father left him with the task of finding water for Old Well Village. Digging wells became his mission in life. The three went straight to the offices of the Well Construction Brigade. They were shunted from one official to another with no effect.

It was a bad day. A visiting geologist was expected, and the office was being spruced up to receive him. No one had time or patience to speak to the three men. Sun Wangquan was not to be put off. He would wait if it took all day.

Just then the visitor arrived, and the staff rushed out to meet him, slamming the door behind them. A new lock with a sensitive dead bolt had just been installed. The door was slammed with such force that the bolt was shot. The office was locked as tight as a box. The visiting dignitary was on the doorstep, and the welcomers were thrown into confusion. One of the younger members of the staff was ordered to climb through a window to unlock the door from the inside. In the confusion no one noticed that Wangquan was still inside. Suddenly the door swung open, and there stood Wangquan, a nervous grin on his face. After that the atmosphere in the office lightened. The geologist was fascinated by tales of Old Well Village: how lack of water led to bloodshed, and how some women bathed thrice in a lifetime. Then and there Geologist Sun decided to visit this typical village in a limestone region.

It was the memory of their unusual first meeting that prompted the geologist's amused grin. With Sun Fuchang leading, the little group wended its way through the village to the west well to examine the stone table. The geologist had expressed an interest in its history.

Geologist Sun walked beside Sun Wangquan, chatting companionably. He had been told that Wangquan was anxious to join the Well Construction Brigade, and remarked that it was not pleasant work.

"I'm not afraid of hard work," said Wangquan. "It would be worth the effort if we find water for the village." He could feel himself blushing even as he spoke. For his motives for joining the

Brigade were not altogether noble. The Brigade represented escape from the drudgery of his life with Xifeng and her mother.

* * *

Xifeng had changed. After she married Wangquan she was the pillar of the household. She toiled from dawn to dusk. No task was too heavy. She was the model wife. Indeed she brought a warmth and tenderness to Wangquan that he had never known.

She was like a flower that wilted in a drought, and then bloomed again after rain. As the days went by, Xifeng recovered the strong character she'd lost after her first husband had been killed. She was the head of the household. Wang Laifu had been a placid man, content to marry into the Duan family and take their name. He had no compunction about being dependent on his wife's family for his livelihood. Wangquan was made of prouder stuff. He resented the undeniable fact that he had lost control of his life. The responsibility of maintaining the household fell on his shoulders yet he had no say in its running. Chores other men would refuse, such as washing clothes and emptying chamber pots, became his daily routine.

His resentment grew. One morning Wangquan rose later than usual. He ignored the chamber pot standing in the middle of the room, wolfed down his morning meal and went down to the fields. When he returned at midday, the aggravating chamber pot had not been moved. He gritted his teeth, hurried through his meal and left again.

Matters came to a head that evening.

Husband and wife and Xiuxiu had just settled round a small table in the courtyard with their evening meal, when Xifeng's mother started ranting in her room.

"Why hasn't the chamber pot been emptied today?" shrilled the woman.

Xifeng scowled violently at Wangquan. He ignored her look and went on eating.

"Mother, can it wait? He's eating."

"Don't you put on airs with me!" her mother shouted back.

Xifeng glared at Wangquan again, and seeing that he was not about to move, whispered, "What are you waiting for? You'll get her all worked up."

This was the breaking point for Wangquan. He turned to her and all the pent up resentment spilled out.

"You do it! Hired hands don't empty chamber pots!"

Xifeng was startled by Wangquan's vehement tone.

"How dare you, Wangquan!" Xifeng's mother kicked open her door. "You don't know when you're well off! I gave you a wife and a decent home, and all of a sudden you're lord mucky-muck! And what's this about 'hired hands'? Are you calling me a landowner? There's a cultural revolution going on you know! I want an apology or you won't hear the end of this!"

Wangquan dashed his bowl to the ground and got to his feet.

"Maybe I don't know when I'm well off. But I damn sure don't want your charity."

He started for the door, but Xifeng grabbed him by the arm.

"Listen to me," she whispered, "my mother went to a lot of trouble arranging this marriage. For the sake of peace let her have her way."

The old woman became even more furious when Xifeng tried to stop Wangquan from leaving.

"Let the untameable beast go!" the woman bellowed. "You can take your rusty old sickle and clear out! But see that I get the marriage settlement back!"

"Mother!" cried Xifeng.

The mother's barb hit home. Wangquan and Xifeng were married during the harvest. Wangquan had been cutting wheat all day. He had come to the wedding straight from the fields. His only possession was a rusty old sickle, because he'd given the few clothes he had to his brother Wanglai.

"I'm leaving! And somehow you'll get back the money you bought me with!"

It was off his chest at last. He felt almost lighthearted. The future was not black any more. He actually sensed hope like a beam of light through heavy clouds. He started to leave again. Xifeng clung to him. She was crying now.

"You can't leave now," she sobbed. "I've missed . . . two months. I'll empty the chamber pot. But please don't leave."

Wangquan stopped, stunned. A child. His child! The world around him darkened again. The blazing ray of hope was gone. Xifeng's mother snapped her mouth shut and retreated into her room.

Now all Wangquan wished for was escape.

* * *

Once the spring rains began there was water in the West Well again, but not enough to supply the village. In a matter of hours the buckets would come up half filled with silt. The well was over sixty feet deep and the rope was long and heavy. It took three or four young people to crank the winch for half a bucket of water. Therefore it was unanimously decided to restrict the use of the well to the hours between daybreak and the morning meal. In this way the well had roughly twenty hours in which to replenish itself for the next day's needs.

"How can you enforce the restriction without a well cover?" Geologist Sun wanted to know.

"That's simple. We lock the winch to put it out of commission," chuckled Sun Fuchang. Then he went on to explain how the rope was attached to the winch with a bucket at each end so that as one was hoisted the other dropped. The geologist made complimentary noises, but he was anxious to see the stone tablet.

"It's right over here," Sun Fuchang led the way. They rounded a corner and came to where the tablet stood. A strange, ragged figure lay on the ground beside the tablet. Except for the twitching of one foot it might have been a scarecrow. Sun Fuchang stopped dead in his tracks, turned to Sun Wangquan and whispered, "It's your crazy uncle. Get rid of him!"

Wangquan reddened. He hurried over to the sleeping figure and shook him.

"It's time to go home, Uncle," he said.

Wanshan sat up with a start, his rheumy eyes rolling wildly. A dirty towel was wrapped around his head with a shock of coarse gray hair bristling out. Around his neck was a garland of willow branches.

"Are they calling me up the mountain again?"

"That's it," said Sun Fuchang trying to keep his voice down. "Your Little Chou is waiting for you up there."

"You're teasing," Wanshan said, his face split in a horrible grin, revealing a row of rotting teeth. Then he noticed the strangers.

"I know what you're up to." He pointed a finger at the outsiders. "You've brought the necromancers to look for water." His voice was suddenly tinged with anger. "They won't find water, because the mountain gods forbid digging wells!"

Wangquan pulled the crazy old man to his feet, half pushed and half dragged him down the lane, still shouting "Nobody will find water! It won't work! It won't work!"

Geologist Sun was already examining the stone tablet. The five foot tall slab had been carved in the third year of Guangxu's reign. The passage of time had done its work, so that the inscription was barely discernible. The geologist adjusted his reading glasses, and laboriously picked out the characters: "History of the great drought at Old Well and Stone Gate."

"Where is Stone Gate?" he asked.

"It's quite a large village not far from here," said Sun Fuchang.

The geologist strained to read the text, when Wanshan leaped in front of the tablet cackling gleefully, "I'm back!"

"This is a good piece of stone," he said, stroking the smooth surface. "But you can't read it without my help."

Before they could seize him, Wanshan slipped out a wet cloth and ran it over the tablet. The text was readable instantly.

"What do you say?" demanded Wanshan triumphantly.

"Thank you sir," the startled geologist stammered.

But Wanshan was not to be put off so easily.

"I've been to the bottom of Hell, and I've pulled down a well!" He fixed the geologist with his mad gaze. "Give us a smoke."

The geologist took out a pack of cigarettes, shook two out and offered them to Wanshan. Wanshan took them both. He stuck one between his lips and tucked the other behind his ear for later. He let the geologist light it for him, and inhaled.

"You've got your cigarette," said Sun Fuchang, barely concealing his impatience.

"Little Chou is waiting on the mountain."

"She's not up there. She's dead." Wanshan's eyes suddenly filled with tears.

"I can hear her singing up there," and Sun Fuchang repeated a few lines of a familiar love song.

Wanshan grew pensive. His head tilted as if he were listening to some distant sound.

"Maybe she is back." A look of wonderment came over him. He trembled. And as suddenly as he appeared he scampered away, the garland of willow branches bobbing gaily round his neck.

The geologist watched him go.

"Who was that?" asked the geologist, a little shaken.

"Just a crazy old man," replied Sun Fuchang blandly.

* * *

Wanshan was the second son of Sun the Mason. He was only a year younger than Wanshui but the two boys were completely different from one another. Both were stone cutters. Whereas Wanshui was bold and hotheaded, Wanshan was a dreamy and gentle youth. He had a deep and lasting love of nature. After a day's work he would come down the mountain with a handful of wild chrysanthemums, or a bunch of red poppies that grew in the gullies. At times he would weave garlands out of green willow branches and drape them around his neck. People used to laugh at him, calling him an incarnation of Jia Baoyu, the hapless young hero of *The Dream of Red Mansions*. He would smile good-naturedly at their gibes, undaunted.

Wanshan grew up with a girl who lived next door who had the curious name of Little Chou, which meant "ugly little thing." Little Chou was pert and pretty. Even as children Wanshan would bring flowers to Little Chou and put them in her hair, or weave garlands to hang around her neck.

As they grew into adulthood Wanshan continued to bring flowers to Little Chou. One day he brought her wild chrysanthemums which she allowed him to put in her hair.

"You're so beautiful," he said, his chest suddenly tight with emotion. "Marry me!"

Little Chou blushed. She plucked at the flowers nervously.

"I won't marry silly old Wanshan," she said with a toss of her head. Her fingers tore at the flowers. He took her hands in his and pinned them behind her back, and drew her towards him. She did not struggle.

"You mustn't destroy beautiful things," he said huskily, and his mouth sought hers.

The next morning Wanshan followed her to the well. Little Chou was more beautiful than ever. She wore a huge wild chrysanthemum behind her ear which drenched her with heady fragrance.

Wanshan turned the winch for her. All the while his heart seemed ready to burst.

"You're so beautiful, Little Chou. Marry me. Please."

The words tumbled out, uncontrollable, and hung in the air between them.

She smiled at him.

"I'm not beautiful, and I won't marry you," she teased.

"Slut!" Little Chou's father's voice shattered their idyll like a clap of thunder. They were so absorbed in each other they had not seen him approach.

Now he stood glaring at them. Little Chou gave a little cry, turned and ran.

The father brushed Wanshan aside, swung the carrying pole on his shoulder and started off.

"Tell you what," he said to Wanshan over his shoulder, "if you can pull down this well, you can have my daughter."

"Pull the well down?" Wanshan repeated the words. "What do you mean?"

"Think about it," said the father, and strode away. Wanshan thought about it long and hard. It was an insoluble riddle. One night he woke with a start, and the simplicity of the solution amazed him. It was impossible to pull the well down, but not impossible to spill its water.

He threw on some clothes, gathered a few tools and ran up to the north well.

At sunrise Little Chou found him hard at work digging a trench.

"What are you doing?" she asked.

Wanshan wiped the sweat off his face and grinned.

"I've found a way to pull down the well ... You're so beautiful ... "

"There you go again!" Little Chou stamped her foot in frustration. "I'll never speak to you again!" She hurried away, her long thick braid of hair slapping against her back.

"I really can knock down the well!" Wanshan shouted after her, but she took no notice.

Wanshan worked on doggedly. At first the villagers scoffed at him, but gradually they saw the logic of what he was doing. Wanshan was digging a trench to connect with the well. Since the trench would be beneath the water level, when the side of the well was penetrated, water would spill into it.

In the meantime, Sun the Mason had died. To Wanshui, the oldest of Sun the Mason's three sons, Wanshan was on a mystic mission just as their father had been. There was a legend in these mountains that the Sung Emperor Zhao Kuangyin passed this way on his journey to the east of the Yellow River. The emperor might have died of thirst had he not found a well. But the well was deep and the emperor had neither rope nor bucket. It is said that the Emperor prayed for divine intervention, and a miracle took place. It happened that the reins of the emperor's horse became tangled in some bushes growing around the well. As the emperor tugged at the reins, trying to free his horse, there was a loud crash. The well tipped over and water came gushing out. Thus man and beast were able to slake their thirst and be on their way. It was this myth that Wanshan was about to duplicate and Wanshui was content to let him do it on his own. Besides, marriage with Little Chou depended upon the success of his enterprise.

Twenty days later Wanshan struck water. The whole village came to see Wanshan's handiwork except Little Chou's father who kept to his house. Wanshan had dug through the side of the well. Now water flowed freely through the opening into the gully. The well had been pulled away. Wanshan busied himself reinforcing the opening. He was soaked to the skin. But he did not mind the discomfort. He was happy. Suddenly there was a rumble. The well caved in and Wanshan was trapped in it.

Wanshui and his remaining brother led the rescue. They took turns, digging round the clock. Finally they found Wanshan curled up at the bottom of the well. There was not a scratch on him. But his eyes were blank, and though his lips moved, he uttered no sound. He was oblivious to his surroundings; even of Little Chou weeping beside the well. He ran up the mountainside as fast as his legs would carry him. Soon his voice raised in song floated down to the village:

The sour plum blossoms are blooming,
And my mother is away . . . love, love, come to me.
The pepper bush is in bloom
And I'm bursting with sweet secrets . . . love
The yam blossoms are drooping
O, how I miss you . . . love . . .
The broom is ready to sweep the kang
There's only you in my heart . . . love . . . "

It was the song Wanshan and Little Chou used to sing to each other as they gathered sour plums in the mountains. It was a sweet, playful ditty. Now it sounded sinister and grotesque. Wanshan had pulled away the well, but he had also gone mad.

* * *

"What an amazing story! And what imagination went into its undertaking!" exclaimed the geologist. He grasped Sun Fuchang's hand and said earnestly, "I should like to see this place!"

The north well was in ruin, and only traces of Sun Wanshan's gully remained. The geologist was deeply moved by this desolate place. But his real concern was for the crazy old man.

"How does he live?" Sun Fuchang was nonplussed.

"Geologist Sun is concerned how you are providing for the old man," explained Zhang, the assistant brigade leader.

"We do what we can," Sun Fuchang shrugged. "He won't eat his rations, and he won't wear the clothes he's issued. He prefers to go about in rags. Ask Wangquan."

"He sleeps wherever he happens to be at nightfall. It might be in a cave or a hay-stack; or maybe on the mountain or down by the river. But he's never sick, and how he gets through the winters without freezing to death is beyond me. In the autumn, when we turn the pigs loose to forage, he follows them, and grabs the yams they dig up. He just dusts them off and gnaws on them, raw. Still he's freer than anybody I know," Wangquan said.

"And what became of his young lady?"

"She's been dead for years," said Sun Fuchang. "She married a man named Hu and went to live in Pingchuan. She had two sons and a daughter, and died very young."

Geologist Sun's face clouded. He turned abruptly and strode up the mountainside. The old geologist was used to mountains. He reached the top of Qinglong Mountain in no time. From this vantage point the whole of Old Well Village lay at his feet. Sun Fuchang pointed out the more than ten wells that the people of Old Well Village had sunk over the years. The dry shafts at the foot of Qinglong Mountain had mostly caved in or been choked by weeds and bushes. Still, some trace of their existence remained. Where there is a heap of rubble there is bound to be an abandoned well nearby, a mute testament of human tenacity in the continuous struggle against nature. The toll in sweat and blood and the heaps of broken stone represent more than anyone could bear to think about.

They lit cigarettes and rested a while, then started back down. Sun Wangquan led the way, and the geologist was surprised and delighted that the route he chose was the one the geologist would have chosen.

"I say, young Sun, why did you choose this route?"

Sun Wangquan reddened.

"There's a layer of red rock that runs through here," stammered Wangquan.

"You seemed to have been following it."

The geologist exchanged knowing glances with his two companions. He stopped, looked about and picked up a rock.

"What sort of stone is this? Is it impervious?"

"It's called red sandstone and it's impervious. If you strike red sandstone as you dig down then you're likely to find water."

"Where did you learn that?"

"I picked it up from a book I read about finding sources of water in mountainous areas."

Sun Fuchang noticed the appreciative gleam in the geologist's eye, and not to be outdone, said, "These youngsters are high school graduates. Now, I've never been to school, but I know a thing or two about rocks also." He pointed to a grayish stone and continued, "That is limestone. It's used to make cement. Although it is impervious, it does not hold water as well."

"You people are remarkable," sighed the geologist.

"There's nothing remarkable about us," said Sun Fuchang matter-of-factly, but there was an unmistakable note of pride in his voice as he continued. "This bit of knowledge we paid for in blood and sweat. Generations of Suns have been stone masons and diggers of wells. I've lost count of the ones that gave their lives searching for water. Only a few months ago Wangquan's father was killed in an accident. That crazy old man we met earlier is Wangquan's uncle."

The Geologist gave Wangquan a look full of sympathy. Wangquan ducked his head in embarrassment, and launched into a description of how the strata of red sandstone ran.

"It's actually right underfoot, but the ravine has cut across it so that it's barely visible from here. But if you look across the ravine to the foot of Wohu Mountain, just beyond that clump of bushes you'll see it quite clearly again. You get a better view of it from the village. I would say it runs a distance of about twelve to fifteen feet. Then it disappears, and you'll only find it on the back of Wohu Mountain."

"What is that?" the Geologist pointed at a jumble of earthenware shards that appeared to be the remains of a pipeline leading down the ravine.

Egg Head, who had not been able to get a word in edgeways, chimed in now.

"That used to be a pipeline," he said, kicking at the shards. "There used to be a small spring up here. At first we used bamboo pipe. But it split due to heat and cold. So we switched to clay pipes, but they weren't much good either."

"Why was that?" the Geologist was interested.

"It just didn't work," Egg Head mumbled, his mind suddenly gone blank.

Wangquan picked up a piece of broken pipe and handed it to Egg Head. For a split second he looked at the length of pipe in his hand blankly. Then something sparked in him.

"That's it!" he cried, "the pipes got plugged with roots!"

The geologist took the piece of pipe from Egg Head and, turning it this way and that, examined it.

"Wasn't cement used to close the joints?" he asked.

Egg Head stuttered something incoherent. Although Sun Fuchang understood the problem he was at a loss to put it into words.

"In these dry hills," began Sun Wangquan, "if there is a leak the size of a pin head, roots will find it."

"That's exactly what I was about to say," Egg Head chirped. "Once roots get into the pipes, they just grow and grow, until the pipe is choked."

"Even plants go mad in these dry hills," sighed the geologist.

It was an opening in the conversation that Engineer Wang was waiting for, and he seized it.

"That is why we have invited you down here. We need your help."

He spoke eloquently of the difficulties the region experienced during the drought two years ago. Most of the region was without water supply. For four months water had to be brought in. Every conceivable vehicle was pressed into service: trucks, tractors, and even donkey carts.

Wang clinched his plea with the statement that the cost of the operation to the state was well in excess of fifty thousand yuan, not to mention the expenditure in labor and wear and tear to machinery.

"I know all that," the geologist responded in his quiet way. "I had first hand experience staying at your county guest house. The first morning there I asked for water to wash my face, and the attendant only smiled and shrugged. Later I found out the taps on the washbasin were only for decoration, and the toilets didn't work either because there was no water supply. I should have been out here long ago."

"But you're here now. It's better late than never!" Zhang Sanhuo put in with a chuckle. "Why not stay a while, and give us some pointers."

"I'll make a deal with you, Old Zhang," replied the geologist earnestly. "You have a few vacancies on the well-digging brigade. I want you to give me two places."

Zhang Sanhuo glanced uneasily at Sun Wangquan and Egg Head, and started to protest.

"You don't have to say yay or nay right this minute," smiled the geologist. "All I ask is that you think it over." He leaned on Wangquan's shoulder and continued softly, "Two high school graduates can't get a job digging wells. Isn't that amazing? What is more amazing is that these young men come from a place where water is scarce. If I were you, I'd put them to good use. Who knows what they might accomplish!"

Suddenly the voice of a man, raised to a cracked and quavering falsetto, came off the slopes of Wohu Mountain singing the song of a young girl gathering sour plums.

The song ended as abruptly as it had begun, and the silence that followed was thunderous.

"Was that the old man?" The geologist's question fell between statement and question.

"It was," countered Sun Fuchang shortly. They were on their way back but the major issue had not been addressed. At last he was compelled to ask the geologist, "What are your thoughts on our water situation?"

"It's hard to make any judgments," the geologist had to admit. "It is almost impossible to give an opinion in a limestone area without a detailed geological study. It will take time, and for that you must rely on your young people."

"You're absolutely right, of course . . . " Sun Fuchang trailed off into silence, trying to summon up a smile.

They walked back in silence, each wrapped in his own thoughts. From time to time the geologist would stop and look back at the mountain they had climbed down. The mountains, the song, and the people troubled him more poignantly than he thought possible.

Far above them a figure emerged from the bushes and climbed laboriously up the ridge of the mountain. There it sat, as if petrified, gazing down at the village, the people and the parched land.

Chapter 7

An Iron Bull 55 tractor, trailing a cloud of dust rumbled towards the mountains along the highway that followed the meandering course of the Qinglong River, carrying water to Old Well Village. The drought was severe in the summer of 1982. Twice a day the tractor traversed the forty odd li that separated Red Stone Hollow from Old Well Village, transporting huge rubber sacks of water. Actually, Red Stone Hollow also lacked water but it happened to be a stop along the narrow gauge railway belonging to the county-operated coal mine. During these hard times, tankers were added to the train and unhitched at various depots. Red Stone Hollow became the supply depot for Old Well Village and several other settlements in the region.

* * *

Sun Wangquan, in a suit of canvas work clothes, with a knapsack on his back, stood swaying to the rhythm of the tractor. His face was covered with a film of yellow grime, making him featureless except for the dull gleam of his eyes. A year ago he and Egg Head joined the county well-digging brigade as part time laborers, mainly through the good offices of Geologist Sun. Egg Head did not stay long. As there was little hope of getting full time employment and the work was hard, life in town soon palled. A month and a half later, Egg Head rolled up his bedding and went home to Old Well Village, to wait for a more suitable opportunity. Sun Wangquan stayed on. A mixture of hope and pain held him fast. He seldom went home during that year. He worked doggedly. At night while his work-mates gambled or drank themselves into a stupor, he buried himself in books, intent on learning all he could about finding water in mountainous regions. The night before, Xifeng had sent him a message saying she was ill, and begging him to go home. Though he was reluctant, his conscience chewed away at him, for Xifeng had been good to him. So he asked for a leave and rushed home. The tractor bumbled along, stirring up a plume of yellowish-gray dust. There had been no snow in the winter, and the spring rains did not come. The Qinglong River was dry, and the sun-bleached pebbles on the river bed were heaped like dried bones under the blazing sky. A few tenacious stalks of corn and sorghum stood in the cultivated patches clinging to the mountainside. But even they began to look discouraged, leaves furled in tight little funnels. The willows along the highway drooped dispiritedly, their leaves turning a dirty gray. The tractor roared and spluttered, and the noise added to the misery of its lone passenger. The dust it kicked up added a gray pall to the summer day that had already lost its greenness.

Sun Wangquan's heart sank as the distance to the village shortened. The misery of life in these dry mountains struck him again.

A flock of sheep and goats were cropping the stubble in the old graveyard near the village when the tractor approached. They pricked up their ears at the familiar rattle. One large ram, bolder than the others, bounded down the slope toward the highway. Instantly the others swarmed after him, filling the roadway. The tractor sputtered and stalled. Sensing the water, instinct drew the animals to the vehicle. Sun Wangquan and the driver Li Sanze leaped off the tractor to beat them back. But the thirst-crazed animals were out of control. Neither shouts nor blows would turn them away. Even the most docile animals became unmanageable in a drought.

One spring when the rains failed, Sun Wangquan was harrowing a field near the old graveyard. At the sound of a tractor approaching the two old oxen pulling the harrow lurched forward with such force that he was yanked sprawling into the dust. The parched animals swerved, and rushed as of one mind toward the approaching tractor and would have collided with it, if one of them had not become tangled in the harness.

As the two men pushed and shoved at the animals to keep them at bay, the splash of water sounded from the back of the tractor. Sun Wangquan turned, and perched on the back of the tractor was the mad old Sun Wanshan gleefully opening the taps on the sacks of water. Wangquan leaped at the old man, and cuffed him soundly. He wrestled the old man off the vehicle and shut off the water. Li Sanze, white with fury, seized the old man and flung him to the ground.

"Why don't you drop dead, you crazy old man!" he bellowed.

"Drop dead yourself!"

The old man picked himself up from the ground and fixed a gummy eye on the driver. "You can't feed animals and not give them a drink!" he replied.

The flock was crowding round the back of the tractor now, greedily sucking at the puddle of muddy water that was fast disappearing into the bone-dry earth. For the moment the road was clear. Li Sanze swallowed the angry words boiling in him, and jumped onto the tractor. The engine kicked back to life, and they went careening down the highway.

Sun Wanshan stood there with the sheep and the goats swarming around him. He took the garland of willow branches from around his neck and tossed it to the animals. He watched them tear it to shreds, clapping his hands and laughing like a child.

The road is all downhill from the old graveyard to the edge of the village. The driver switched off the engine, and let the tractor coast down the slope. Even so, the villagers were ready with their buckets. A ragged and noisy queue formed quickly behind the tractor before it came to a standstill. Buckets clattered. People shouted at each other. The din was deafening. No one paid much attention to Wangquan. For that matter he was hardly noticed except for the shy smiles of recognition a few young girls flashed at him.

It was the season of ration coupons again. People came with the precious bits of paper clenched between their lips or clutched in the palms of their hands. Water was rationed whenever there was a severe drought and it had to be brought in. A family of six or more was allowed four bucketfuls; a family of three or more, two buckets; a couple was allowed one, and a single person, half a bucket. It was all the water that a tractor could transport in two trips a day.

Sun Wangquan fought his way through the milling crowd. The sun-baked earth and the thirsting people it spawned oppressed him. He ducked his head and hurried home, grim-faced, a bitter line creasing the corners of his clenched lips.

"Wangquan, you're home!" cried Sun Fuchang coming out of his door, buckets in hand. "No use hurrying home. You're not climbing on her today. So stop a moment. I have something to tell you."

They stood on the street corner, lit cigarettes and smoked in silence. Sun Fuchang searched Wangquan's narrow face. He coughed portentously and started in. "I went to town the other day to see old Wang of the water authority, to ask for help in locating a well. You know what he said?" Sun Fuchang paused for effect. "He said that we have an expert in our midst." He paused again, his eyes never straying from Wangquan's face. "And that expert is you. He says you've read dozens of books on the subject, and you've been to a three-month course. What's more, he says you've accurately located wells for other villages. Is that true?"

Wangquan bowed his head. For a moment he said nothing.

"It's true," he said, finally, looking Sun Fuchang straight in the eye. "But our village stands on limestone. And where there's limestone, water is hard to find."

"Hard to find," echoed Sun Fuchang. "Does that mean it's hopeless . . . " His voice trailed off, and his face clouded.

Wangquan turned away. He could not bear the look of bitterness and disappointment on his uncle's face.

"What do you think of the new policy of responsibility?" Sun Fuchang's thoughts seemed to have taken a different tack, and the words spilled out on their own. "Do you think it will work?" Wangquan, we are family, so let's be honest with each other. The land has already been distributed. Soon I won't have to worry about the village any more."

So you're afraid of losing authority, thought Wangquan, but haven't you had enough?

Still he said nothing.

The older man went on in a monotone.

"I don't mind stepping down. I've been branch secretary for almost twenty years. In that time, I've built a commune, dug ditches, worked on a dam and dredged the west well. There's just one more thing I want to do before I go." Sun Fuchang lifted his eyes to Wangquan, and there was pleading in his voice. "Wangquan, help me sink a well before I step down. It will be my legacy to the village, so that when I die, I will not have lived in vain."

Wangquan trembled inwardly. His uncle's words struck a deep chord. For the first time in his life, he noticed a glimmer of moisture in Sun Fuchang's hooded and lusterless eyes.

"While I still have the authority, I'm going to depend entirely on your judgment. You and I will give it a good try. I don't believe that in all the world we stand on the only corner that has no water. The village may have to tighten its belts for a few years. We'll sink another well. If it turns out to be another dry shaft then the village is doomed. If we succeed, the village will raise a tablet to commemorate your achievement." He paused, then added, "The village will raise a tablet whether we succeed or not," he took one more drag on his cigarette and flicked the butt away. "If we fail, the tablet will serve warning to those who come after us not to squander their lives in this desolate place."

The blood was running fast and heavy through Wangquan's veins. He thought of his father's blighted life, and his eyes burned with tears. He turned and quickly walked away.

"Wangquan, for heaven's sake, say something," pleaded Sun Fuchang.

"I'll go to the bottom of hell with you," Wangquan shouted, looking back over his shoulder. He quickened his step, his throat so constricted he could hardly breathe. The tears he fought to hold back made muddy little trails down his face. He wept for his father—his mad uncle—his grandfather. He wept for all the nameless generations of Suns who gave their lives digging well. He wept for himself and he vowed that if he succeeded, the first bowl of water would be dedicated to the spirits of all those who had gone before him.

* * *

Sun Wangquan's head was bursting as he hurried home. The task that lay ahead fired his imagination and gave a new spring to his step.

The child, Xiuxiu, was making mud pies outside the gate. Wangquan hailed her from a distance, and the child ran into the yard to tell her grandmother that her father was home.

Xifeng's mother was scrubbing a pile of clothes when Wangquan stepped through the gate. There was such an air of contentment about the woman that he was taken aback. The old woman dried her hands, and came to greet him, beaming from ear to ear.

"The man of the house is back," she cried, and for once she seemed genuinely pleased to see him. Nevertheless he was distrustful.

Aloud he said, "What is the matter with Xifeng?"

"What could be the matter? She's a woman, and she had a bit of pain in the stomach."

Stomach pains. The words did not penetrate just then, but he quickened his step toward his rooms. He sensed a change in his surroundings, but his mind was still so packed full of the future that it could not focus on the present. He lifted the curtain that hung in his doorway. Vaguely he noticed something red had been stitched to it that hadn't been there before. A soft but insistent mewing sound came from within. A newborn baby! He tiptoed towards the inner room, his knees trembling. He lifted the curtain in the doorway, and there in the middle of the kang lay a tiny bundle.

The reality of a child had not registered in his mind until that moment.

Xifeng reclined on a mound of quilts, her hair tied in a blue and white checkered cloth.

"You're back," she smiled at him softly.

Wangquan peered at the tiny bundle on the kang.

"When did it happen?"

"In the night." She was pale, her face puffy. "The impatient little thing couldn't wait for his father to get home." She looked at the child as though she could never get enough of seeing him. "Look at that little nose, and that little mouth. He has my eyes, but your mouth."

Wangquan gazed at the child in wonderment.

"Boy? Or girl?"

"Didn't you notice how happy my mother is?" the woman teased, chuckling delightedly. "It's a boy, of course. Here, I'll show you." She took the child, and unwrapped it for Wangquan to see, crooning softly, "Don't you cry, my beautiful fat son—Here's your father, my precious one."

A son. My son. Wangquan's eyes misted. He buried his face in the woman's shoulder. He did not think it possible, but the child made him feel a sudden change, a new meaning pouring into his life, his home and his woman. He was overwhelmed with gratitude and remorse. Gratitude for what she had given him; remorse for his long indifference to her.

Xifeng sensed the conflict in Wangquan. She lifted her face to his, pressing her cheek against his. The faint pressure of flesh against flesh sent a tingle through him. He took her face between his hands and kissed her mouth, her nose, her cheeks, again and again. At first she squirmed and giggled, then she became quiet. She tried to smile, but tears rolled down her cheeks instead. Her arms went around his neck, and she held him with all her strength. She was crying hard now, her body shaking with deep sobs. She wept for her wasted womanhood mostly but also for the men in her life. One was dead, and the other a placid captive who had never given her the emotion she longed for.

There was a movement at the door, and Xifeng quickly pushed Wangquan from her.

It was Xiuxiu, standing there wide-eyed.

Wangquan beckoned the child to him.

"Look what your father brought you," he said, undoing his knapsack. There was a packet of fruit drops, a picture book and a packet of biscuits. He laid the presents on the edge of the kang. The child took a handful of fruit drops and went out again.

Xifeng felt cleansed by the tears. Her mood lightened. She patted the kang beside her, and Wangquan sat close to her. She smiled up at him through red-rimmed eyes.

"The baby needs a name. But mother says he has to take my father's family name. Duan." She looked at him fearfully.

Wangquan nodded in agreement. After all it was part of the marriage contract.

"The first character in the name was decided by my mother," Xifeng said, relieved that Wangquan raised no objections. "I thought your family name Sun should be included too. So the second character is my choice. You've read so much. Choose a good character from one of your books to round it off."

"Let it be 'Jing' for well," Wangquan decided. "It's practical. In a place like this, having a well is a matter of life and death. If we have a well we have everything, and life will go on and on."

"Then it's settled," Xifeng smiled. "All my mother could think of was my father's family name; and all I could think of was my man's. And all you think of is digging wells, like your ancestors. I'm afraid you might turn into a well yourself, and our son too." She spoke the child's name, Duan Sunjing, rolling it off her tongue, savoring it.

"Doesn't it sound awkward?" she asked doubtfully.

"Once you get used to it, it'll sound just fine," Wangquan said.

Xifeng tucked a stray strand of hair under her headcloth, and picked up the baby, cuddling it and crooning softly, "You're wet again, my little sprout. But don't you cry. You have a proper name now, my little Jing."

Wangquan slipped out of the room, and headed for Qinglong Mountain. He was going to find water. He was determined to succeed where generations of men from Old Well Village had failed. Earlier when he spoke with Sun Fuchang, he had decided to take on the task for the sake of his forefathers. His son changed all that. He was doing it now, not only for the dead, but for his son, and his son's sons, and countless generations to come. He had vowed to dedicate the first bowl of water to his ancestors. Instead, he would offer it to his son. Little Jing would grow into manhood and find himself a woman and have children. A well insured that continuity. He was exhilarated and filled with a sense of mission that he had never felt before. From the top of the mountain he could see the village and his home. How small they looked, yet how precious.

* * *

Sun Wangquan covered more than ten li of mountain paths that day. He had scaled peaks and gone down ravines. By afternoon he was tired and parched. He made his way back up the mountain, intending to drink his fill at a spring before starting home. But the spring had dried up. There was nothing to do but start down swallowing his saliva. As he rounded a bend in the path, Wangquan caught a flash of a woman carrying a pair of food containers disappear behind a clump of trees. This was not unusual in the mountains, where women often carried the midday meal to their menfolk working in the fields five and ten li from home. By the woman's steady, balanced movement Wangquan could tell that the big food jars she carried were probably full of water and she was on her way home. The women usually stopped at a spring to wash out the containers and fill them with water. A moment later he saw her come out of the grove, and he shouted after her. She gave no sign that she heard him, and slipped quickly out of sight. The village was still some distance away, and the thought of cool spring water tantalized him.

Wangquan hurried after her.

"I say, can you spare a drink of water?" he croaked, his dry tongue sticking to his palate.

He found her resting in the shade of a large boulder. She had leaned her carrying pole against the rock. Her two black earthenware jars sat in the middle of the path. It was Qiaoying.

Wangquan never thought he would see her alone again, and coming on her like this left him stunned.

Qiaoying left the village the night his marriage was agreed on. She went to the city and stayed with her father for six months. By the time she returned, he had joined the well-digging brigade. Some say Qiaoying came back because there was no work for her in the city. Others say she came back because she could not forget Wangquan. Aside from that everyone agreed that Qiaoying had become more foreign than before. It was not just the clothes she wore, or the way she spoke and carried herself, it even showed in her work. People advised her against growing peanuts and cotton on her self-owned land, saying she would never manage the fields on her own. But she turned a deaf ear to their well-meant advice. Indeed she never touched a hoe after the soil was broken. Weed killers kept her fields tidier than those of farmers who labored from dawn to dusk. Even the tedious task of pinching off side shoots of cotton plants was done by spraying chemicals.

Qiaoying was definitely not a typical farm woman, and the villagers viewed her achievements with a mixture of envy and suspicion. But the test of the pudding is in the eating, the villagers muttered among themselves, and the reckoning for her foolishness would come at harvest time. For Qiaoying spent less time in her fields than it took her to get there. A handful of chemical fertilizer here, and a spray of insect repellent there, and her work was done.

When she was home, Qiaoying did not stitch shoes or mend clothes. She drew some chalk lines on the ground in front of her house, and strung up a net, and taught the young people a game called badminton.

The sight of young men and women batting a little bunch of feathers back and forth was another thorn in the side of the old folk.

Wangquan had witnessed a game of badminton one time when he came home. A noisy bunch of young people were gathered outside Qiaoying's door, laughing and chattering, watching a game. Wangquan tried to pass without being noticed, but Egg Head spotted him.

"Wangquan, come and play," he crowed, "Qiaoying's beaten all of us! You've got to help us out!"

The others looked from Wangquan to Qiaoying. If she noticed him at all, Qiaoying certainly gave no indication, except to swat the shuttlecock with extra force. That day she had on a sleeveless white blouse. Her face was flushed and beaded with sweat. Her firm young breasts rose and fell with every breath, exuding youthful vitality. Wangquan waved Egg Head aside, and walked away with an awkward smile. The badminton games stopped not long afterwards. Perhaps the novelty wore off. More likely it was simply that after toiling in the fields all day, no one had the energy for badminton. The old folk who grumbled that Qiaoying did not conform to their ideas of rural womanhood whispered sagely among themselves, "We've been a village for almost a thousand years but things haven't changed much. We've seen cooperatives, communes, agricultural education camps come and go. They all tried to change things. But somehow things stay the same. And here's a young woman who wants to change the way of life of the country people. Well, it's easier said than done."

Wangquan and Qiaoying did not seek each other out. On the rare occasions when they met each other on the street, one or the other would cross to the other side. Qiaoying moved with the same firm stride, her shoulders back, her head held high. She was getting on with her life. Wangquan comforted himself with that thought.

Perhaps she had heard him call out after all. Zhao Qiaoying turned her head, gave him a sidelong glance and looked away again. Wangquan was breathing hard. He looked at the food containers on the ground regretfully and turned to go.

"Does your conscience bother you that much, or aren't you thirsty?" her voice cut like a knife.

Wangquan stopped and faced her. Qiaoying had taken up one of the containers, poured half a bowl of water and was holding it up to him.

"Do I have to bring it to you?"

Wangquan took the bowl from her and lifted it to his lips. With one swift movement Qiaoying tore the kerchief off her head. A little cloud of dust, grass seeds and twigs flew in the air, and quickly settled in the bowl of water. Wangquan wondered dully whether she had done it deliberately. He lifted the bowl again blowing gently across the surface of the water to clear it, taking tiny sips. The water was sweet and icy cold. He would have gulped it down, had it not been for the bits of debris floating in it. Slowly he drained the bowl. But half a bowl was not enough. He wanted more. Wordlessly he held out the bowl to her, hoping she would take the hint, and fill it again. She took the bowl, clamped it on her food container and left without a backward glance.

Let it be, he thought to himself. Let it go. It's water under the bridge now. No use thinking about it.

A snatch of a mountain song came out of the distance:

The sorghum stands tall in the field;
My troubles are your doing, Brother.
Wild iris blooms on the wayside;
Where is your heart, Brother . . .

Wangquan threw himself down on a patch of wild flowers. He had done his grandfather's bidding, provided for his brother, and gave the Duan family an heir. But in accomplishing that he injured the only woman who loved him with all her being. He had a cause, and he had a son. He thought they would fulfill him and give him peace. But seeing Qiaoying again stirred up all the old emotions he knew he could never escape.

Qiaoying, carrying her containers, moving with her quick light step, was soon hidden by clumps of brambles, scrub pine and golden broom that clung stubbornly to the mountainside and the ravines. A hot dry wind moaned. The song trailed off into silence. Perhaps it was drowned by the wind, or perhaps the singer grew tired.

Chapter 8

At the back of Old Well Village, near a place called Pine Creek, there is a fairly large pond. The pond, which measures about ten meters square, snuggles against the western foot of Qinglong Mountain. A gully joins it to Pine Creek. In this way, the overflow from Pine Creek is channeled into the pond after heavy rain.

In the mountains, ponds such as this are sometimes called hemp pools. After harvesting, hemp stalks are tied in bundles and laid at the bottom of the pond. Weighed down by rocks, the hemp is left to soak until the greenness has gone out of the stalks. Only then can the fibers be extracted. The ponds are public property, meaning that everyone in the village or commune uses it to wash clothes, soak hemp or water their cattle. However, only animals bred in the mountains would drink the greenish black water of the pond. Animals brought in from outside would only drink it in desperation, and even then they would lap at it warily. Those who care for their new cattle would mix pond water with fresh water for the first month, until the animals got used to it. But no human could drink from the pond and not be sick within an hour.

On the mountainside, some distance above the pond there used to stand a huge boulder, the size of a small house. One summer when the Agricultural Study Camp was still in existence, it was decided to remove the boulder by blasting. Some women were washing clothes in the pond one day, when they were startled by a great roar, and looking up, saw the rock hurtling towards them. The women scattered. The rock finally came to rest in the middle of the pond. Some cattle were tethered close by. The frightened beasts broke their harnesses and bolted, and for weeks after, could not be forced to go near the pond. The day after the explosion, all was serene. In time the rock became covered with moss, and an elm tree sprouted from a crevice and the pond became a scenic spot in drab Old Well Village.

The lives of Sun Wangquan and Zhao Qiaoying, like the pond, gradually settled into some semblance of serenity. After their encounter on the mountain, when she had given him water, they spoke with each other whenever they met. Their nervous casual conversation never touched upon the past. But like the animals who gradually become accustomed to the brackish water of the pond, it was merely a question of time.

That same day Wangquan began searching the mountains for a well site. Determining a site in a limestone belt was a daunting task even for the experts. Thus Sun Wangquan carefully kept his own council, working on the project on his days off, which were not many. There was a dearth of geological material, and only his two school friends, Egg Head and Qiaoying, who knew something of algebra and geometry, could help with the basic calculations. So the two were persuaded to join him. Wangquan went home whenever he could. He would throw down his gear, pack some food and water, and be off again, roaming the mountains.

Zhao Qiaoying still dreamed of the world beyond the mountains. She had no interest in wells. But she went along for Wangquan's sake.

"What are you doing, running up the mountain and down the ravines?" she asked.

"I go to the high points to examine the terrain," he said. "I go down the ravines to study the rock strata left by old creeks and streams."

"Don't you want to be with your wife?" she persisted.

Wangquan would redden, mutter some excuse and walk away.

In spite of herself, Qiaoying had to admire Wangquan's dedication. She hated him, yet she loved him still; and she wanted to help him in his undertaking.

As for Egg Head, Sun Wangcai was even less interested in wells. With his father's connections he could get a job of some description if he put his mind to it. But he was passive and lazy, content to let opportunity seek him. Egg Head went along partly for Wangquan's sake but mainly to be near Qiaoying. Pretty and aloof, she would not give him a second glance. But away from the village she was different. She chatted and laughed at his crude jokes. But the best was when they reached the more difficult sections and had to climb, and she would allow him to grab her wrist and give her a pull, or give her a boost with his hands on her waist. He was careful not to pinch, and sometimes she would reward him with a smile. When they stopped for food, Egg Head would watch Qiaoying eat. After she had drunk from the canteen, he would press it to his lips and suck on it as noisily as he could. When Qiaoying took no notice, he would put down the canteen with a sigh. "The canteen is luckier than I," he said wistfully. "It got to kiss you."

And Qiaoying would call him a devil, but he could see she was not really annoyed. Though she gave him no encouragement, Egg Head was grateful to Qiaoying for the crumbs of attention she scattered his way.

The seasons passed into winter. Armed with instruments crudely assembled out of bits and pieces of old compasses and sextants, and a surveyor's pole, Wangquan and his friends covered every nook and cranny around Old Well Village. Wangquan learned all that he could about the terrain, the nature of the soil, and the depths of the water table. Out of all this information, he worked out a location and a design for the well. Finally he was ready to present his scheme to Sun Fuchang, who accepted it with glee. It was decided then and there that work would begin as soon as winter set in, and the farmers were freed from their fields. The county well-digging brigade seconded Wangquan to lead the work crew at Old Well Village, hoping thus to benefit from his experiences, and eventually to lift the prohibition against sinking wells in limestone regions.

Two months after the work began, Wangquan discovered some discrepancies between his calculations and the actual soil he was encountering. Deeply troubled, he decided to quietly make another survey. According to his calculations there ought to have been a water table about two hundred meters from the mouth of Pine Creek. He tried to follow the fault but lost it somewhere between Qinglong and Wohu mountain. If he could locate that fault, then he could feel more confident about the position of the well.

One bitterly cold winter's day, with a sharp gale blowing, Qiaoying and Wangquan strapped the surveying equipment on their backs, and hiked up Qinglong mountain. It was not until almost sunset that they thought they spotted a trace of what they were looking for.

They were on a westward-facing precipice known as Pancake Cliff. It is said a rock dropped from the top would take the same length of time to hit bottom as a man would take to eat a pancake. As the cliff also forms part of the boundary between Shanxi and Hebei provinces, local wits have dubbed it the shortest route to Hebei. Jump off the cliff and you're there. Perhaps Pancake Cliff's principal claim to fame was the memory of a pitched battle during the Sino-Japanese war. The Eighth Army was trapped on the cliff. The battle raged for a day and into the night. When it was over most of the men were dead.

The precipice was covered with brambles and sour plum bushes, but faint traces of the fault could be seen running along the face of the cliff.

As they followed the fault along the top of the cliff, Qiaoying was startled by a movement among the bushes. A small fox came out of its burrow and bounded across the clearing. Qiaoying ran after it. The little fox ran and stopped as if it were deliberately leading its pursuer on, until it finally disappeared into a thicket at the edge of the clearing.

"Come back, vixen, it's getting late," shouted Wangquan. His old nickname for Qiaoying had slipped out, and she was quick to pick up on it.

"I'm a fox fairy," she countered, as she came panting back to where he stood waiting, her face chafed by the wind, glowing.

They stepped gingerly to the edge of the cliff and looked down into the yawning abyss already shrouded in darkness. Qiaoying gave a little cry of fright and clung to Wangquan's arm. They stepped back, and lying flat on the ground inched their way to the edge and linking hands, looked down again. With his free hand, Wangquan found a stone and dropped it over the side. It seemed a long while before the sound of it striking the foot of the cliff echoed up to them. Qiaoying found a rock the size of a rice bowl, and timing its fall on her watch, sent it over the side. She counted the seconds till the sound of it hitting bottom traveled up.

"Eight seconds" she murmured. The formula for free-falling objects—$\frac{1}{2}Gt^2$—flashed through her mind.

"Eight seconds ... that makes it three hundred and twenty meters," she said aloud.

"If it's over three hundred meters, you ought to take off one second for the sound to travel up. That makes it seven seconds. Let's say it's just under three hundred meters."

"It's at least three hundred meters," Qiaoying insisted, annoyed that Wangquan's calculation might be more accurate than hers. "It was eight seconds before we heard the stone strike bottom. It has to be at least three hundred meters."

"All right, have it your way," Qiaoying's sudden flash of childish temper made Wangquan smile. Wangquan eyed the cliff face, muttering that he still could not see the fault clearly.

"Maybe you'll get a better view from over there," suggested Qiaoying. She had gotten over her initial fear of heights. She let go of Wangquan's hand and moved away in the direction she had indicated.

He did not try to stop her, nor did he look to see where she was going, until he heard the rumble of falling sand and rocks. The edge of the cliff had fallen away and taken Qiaoying with it.

Wangquan scrambled to his feet and raced to the spot where Qiaoying had been moments ago. Getting on hands and knees, he looked over the jagged edge of a hole where a large rock had been dropped into the black void below. Something exploded in Wangquan's brain. He gripped the edge of the cliff with both hands and let out a wild, desperate cry.

"Qiaoqiao! Qiaoqiao!"

From below a tremulous voice answered, "Help me ... Wangquan ... help me."

Wangquan's brain cleared. He looked down again. The root of a tree jutting out of the cliff broke Qiaoying's fall. She managed to grab hold of it with one hand as she slid past. She hung by one hand pressed against the rock face, while with her free hand she groped for a crevice, a root, anything at all to hang on to.

"Hurry please ... I can't hang on much longer," she cried.

Wangquan examined the cliff face, fighting to keep calm. He could see a narrow ledge beneath Qiaoying's feet. It was less than half a meter wide. One could stand on it quite comfortably near the ground. But at that height and in a brisk wind it was a dangerous, paralyzing foothold. Still it was a chance.

Wangquan cleared his throat and spoke in a tone usually reserved for coaxing small children.

"Qiaoqiao ... listen to me. I know you can't see your feet, but you're actually on a ledge. Now don't look down. Just do what I say. Move your foot sideways a third of a meter." Seeing that she would not follow his directions, Wangquan took a different tack. "There's a ledge just above you. Grip it with your left hand!" He held his breath while her left hand groped for the ledge, and found it. "Now move your foot sideways. See how easy it was! Just a little further ... "

A cold sweat was pouring down Wangquan's face, but for the moment Qiaoying was safe.

"I'll run to the village for some rope," he said.

"Don't leave me," Qiaoying pleaded, an edge of panic in her voice.

"I won't leave you," Wangquan comforted her, all the while searching for a way to reach her.

"My legs are getting numb," Qiaoying cried, "I can't hold on much longer. You've wasted my life, Wangquan, but I love you ... I don't want to let you go ... "

Wangquan's eyes brimmed. Even with life and death dangling on a thread, she would think of love. His mouth was so dry he couldn't squeeze out a word. Frantically he looked for a way either to haul her up or to climb down to her. He knew that with him near her, Qiaoying would hold on. Otherwise her courage would fail and she would fall. Finally he spotted a ledge near Qiaoying, and a way to climb down. For the moment he did not stop to think what to do next. He was intent on reaching the ledge. He called out to Qiaoying that he was coming for her and started climbing down. It was not difficult at first, but soon turned treacherous. There were no footholds, and he began to slip. By then he was a scant half meter above the ledge. Wangquan pressed against the face of the cliff and allowed himself to slide gently onto the ledge. But as his feet touched ground, his knees bent, and hit the rock face. He lost his balance and felt himself falling backwards. The abyss yawned below. Suddenly a gnarled scholar tree growing out of the cliff swam into view. With the courage of desperation, Wangquan launched himself at it. Next moment his arms were wrapped around the tree trunk. The impact had knocked the breath from him. When he regained his breath he found that the tree was firmly anchored in a crevice, and directly under it was a wide ledge, covered with tufts of dry grass. This ledge was lower than the first. Still clinging to the tree he could make out what appeared to be a footpath.

Qiaoying was still spread-eagled against the cliff. Fortunately she had not seen his near disaster, nor had he cried out, or she might have been startled into falling.

Wangquan caught his breath and called out to Qiaoying.

"I've found a good spot. It's the size of a room. I can't go to you, so you have to come to me. It's only five or six meters away."

"I can't move! I'm scared!" Qiaoying pressed herself against the rock face, barely breathing.

"You'll freeze if you stay out there much longer," Wangquan was anxious now.

His voice dropped to a gentle coaxing tone. "Hold on tight with your left hand. Move your right hand a half meter to your right. Get a good grip on the crevice there. Now shift your right foot half a step."

Qiaoying inched her way along the face of the cliff. After the first few steps it became easier. Slowly she reached the small ledge where he fell earlier.

"Qiaoqiao, get a tight grip, then turn towards me."

Qiaoying turned her head slowly, and when she saw Wangquan clinging to the tree she screamed from fear.

"It's all right. I'm going to drop down on the big ledge below me. Then you'll have to jump too." With that he dropped lightly onto the grassy ledge.

"I can't jump!" Qiaoying forced the words out through chattering teeth. "If I miss I'll end up in Hebei."

"What was your record for the standing long jump at school?" asked Wangquan.

"Two meters," said Qiaoying, wondering what he was driving at.

"Well, this isn't quite one and a half. You can do it. Besides, it's getting dark. Are you going to hang there all night?

Qiaoying could see she had no other choice. She gritted her teeth and jumped. Wangquan caught her as she landed, and the two fell to the ground in a heap. Qiaoying's aloofness and Wangquan's reserve were shattered by their narrow escape. Qiaoying clung tightly to Wangquan, weeping hysterically. He rocked her in his arms until she quieted down.

"Let me see if there's a way out, before it gets dark," Wangquan tried to disengage himself. But she kept holding him tight, her teeth still chattering. He gathered her into his arms again, crooning to her as if she were a small child.

Night falls quickly in the mountains. That night they were stranded on the mountain. Sun Wangquan gathered an armful of dry grass and twigs and built a fire against the side of the cliff, and they huddled over the flame trying to keep warm. Now that they were relatively safe, the barriers between them went up again, and neither knew what to say to the other.

An icy wind blew across Pancake Cliff, whistling and moaning among the craggy outcroppings of rock, and rustling the grass and low brush. Sun Wangquan gathered grass to make a pallet for Qiaoying. In one corner of the ledge was a pile of rubble where sand and stones had fallen from the top of the cliff. Thinking this was a promising spot, Wangquan started to clear away some of the debris. Clawing through it he uncovered a small hole. He flipped a stone in it, and the sound of the stone rolling suggested a cave. He began digging in earnest then, and behind the rubble found an opening. He lit a bunch of dry grass and by its flickering light saw that it was indeed a cave with a flat floor; a perfect shelter for the night. Wangquan lit another handful of grass and holding it up, guided Qiaoying into the cave.

The cave was much larger than he expected. A few feet from the entrance was a tangle of wheels and rusty metal rods, and parts of machinery. In a corner were wooden crates containing parts of firearms and field artillery pieces. They had stumbled upon the remains of the only battle fought in this region during the war.

"Who do these belong to?" Qiaoying wondered. The rust, the cobwebs and the dust made it obvious that no one had been in the cave for a long time.

"It probably belonged to the Eighth Army," said Wangquan. "My grandfather used to tell of a secret ammunition dump in these mountains. He said he used to see convoys going in and out of these mountains with huge wooden crates. Nobody knew where they came from, or where they were going."

The bunch of grass was rapidly burning down. Wangquan tore a few rotting planks from the crates, piled them up and set them ablaze. He soon had a crackling fire burning. Then he piled some rocks across the entrance of the cave as a wind break, and made a pallet of dry grass beside the fire for Qiaoying. The dankness soon went out of the air, and the narrow cave became snug and almost cheerful. They huddled over the fire to keep warm.

"In the morning we'll find a way out," Wangquan reassured Qiaoying.

"I don't want to think about tomorrow," Qiaoying poked moodily at the fire with a stick, "as long as I have this night with you."

Wangquan reddened.

"I thought you hated me," he said without looking at her. "You wouldn't even give me a drink of water that day on the mountain."

Qiaoying gave him a sidelong glance.

"I must have given half a bowl of water to a stray dog that day," she said.

"It was pretty underhanded, the way you scattered dirt and twigs on the water," Wangquan added bitterly.

"Stupid man," flashed Qiaoying. She poked Wangquan's forehead.

"It was a very hot day, and the water was icy. You might have gotten cramps if you gulped it down. Don't you remember what happened to Laoer's wife? I scattered a bit of dust so you had to blow it away and take small sips. It was the only way to keep you from guzzling the water."

Sun Wangquan bowed his head. He thought of the bowl of cold spring water, with the flecks of dirt and grass floating in it. And he thought of the almond shaped eyes fixed on him with tenderness and misery. And he heard again her song of reproach.

"Hey," she gave him a jab with the stick in her hand, "you were almost rid of me today."

"What are you saying?" Wangquan looked at her, astonished.

"Your grandfather waved a sod chopper at you, and you dropped me like a hot brick."

It was a stain on his conscience that all the water of the Yellow River could not wash away.

Wangquan tried to explain that he had no choice. They could not marry without parental approval. His grandfather threatened suicide, and Qiaoying's father had been recalled to his job in the city.

"You would never be content to stay in the village. So I married into the Duan family. That way my brother could have a proper marriage, and you would be free to pursue your dreams." Even as he spoke, he realized how senseless and hollow his words sounded.

"Excuses. Nothing but excuses," Qiaoying cried bitterly.

Suddenly he was angry.

"I went looking for you that night, but you'd gone. What did you do all those months?"

"What was there to do?" she countered. "I ate a little; drank a little. I walked the streets; I went to bed. You didn't want me and I wasn't going to beg." She turned to him, eyes black with bitterness. "I had your son scraped out of me."

Wangquan could not meet her gaze. He picked up a piece of wood and tossed it on the fire, and watched it crackle into flame.

"How could you tell it was a boy?"

"A woman senses these things," Qiaoying said simply. She hugged her knees, rocking gently back and forth, the tears glistening on her cheeks in the firelight. "I wanted to give you a son so much."

Wangquan pressed his forehead against her knees, caught in a spiral of remorse, humility, sadness and despair.

Qiaoying gently brushed the dust from his shoulders, and stuffed the cotton back into the rip in his jacket. Silent tears tumbled down her cheeks. After awhile she sighed, "It's all in the past now. It's life."

She stroked his shoulders absently.

Suddenly she laughed.

"We're a fine pair. You look so silly on your knees!"

She drew him tenderly to her.

"Lie with me . . . and talk to me."

Sun Wangquan shrank from her warmth and busied himself with the fire. A shadow passed over Qiaoying's face. She lay down and turned her face into the straw of the pallet. She lay perfectly still with her back to him. When Wangquan did not move, she turned on her back, and shifted her body to one side.

"Wangquan, do I have to beg?"

Wangquan stood, petrified. The woman lying on the pallet was everything he wanted, but he belonged to the Duan family now.

Qiaoying glared at him angrily and turned away. Suddenly her eyes snapped wide. Slowly she sat up, her face pale with horror. Wangquan gathered her in his arms, his gaze following hers. Under the rusty machinery lay a skeleton.

The bleached white bones were covered with a film of dust. Someone had carefully laid out the corpse. A porcelain bowl and a rusty rifle were laid beside it.

Qiaoying's eyes were wide with terror.

"Is it a rifle?"

"It is," replied Wangquan.

Qiaoying shut her eyes and snuggled against Wangquan.

"And there's a porcelain bowl too," she shuddered. "Wangquan, we'll never get out of this place."

Wangquan laid her gently on the pallet, and stretched out beside her, holding her close. A cold little hand crept under his shirt and wandered across his thick, hard muscles. Her fingertips were on a mysterious quest.

He looked deep into her eyes.

"Let me see it again," she whispered.

He opened his shirt, and she pressed her lips against the blood red birthmark that ran all the way down the middle of his chest.

"Are you really the reincarnation of Sun Xiaolong?"

"And are you really a fox fairy?" He tried to make a joke of it, but the sadness in her eyes made him falter.

"Maybe I really am a fox fairy," she whispered. "That night when the Third Auntie cast her spell, I could feel it in all my bones. The little fox on top of the cliff was trying to lead us away from harm."

"I don't care if you are a fox fairy," he said thickly. "I love you."

His eyes were shining now. Slowly she undid her blouse, and unhooked her pale green brassiere. Her firm young breasts leaped out at him, and pressed against the hardness of his chest. Her lips sought his hungrily. His heart contracted.

A chill ran up his spine, and turned into a raging fire at the back of his skull. He drew her to him, as if he were holding life itself.

"We'll die here . . . together . . . "

"No, Qiaoqiao . . . "

The fire was a pile of glowing embers now. In the gathering darkness the bonds of death were loosened. He felt himself melt into her. That wild torrent of life, dammed up too long, burst within him. He was swept along on a wave of passion that carried him to the brink of death and beyond.

"Let me die . . . let me die . . . "

She cried out once. They floated apart. He seemed to drift in a swirling fog. He seemed to lose all sense of himself.

Slowly he opened his eyes. The fire was a heap of graying ashes. He shifted his body, and her arms tightened around him immediately, drawing him into her again. His hand cupped one breast and squeezed until she cried out. He was suffused with her warmth and her tenderness. Vaguely he wondered why he had not married Qiaoying; why he had allowed himself to be bought like a slave by the Duans. He wondered whether he could face the life he led, and what would become of all of them.

"What are we going to do?" he whispered.

She said nothing at first, then she whispered the lines of a song about brave doomed lovers.

Her eyes were shining in the darkness. His arms slipped around her, and he took her again.

Chapter 9

When Sun Wangquan did not come home by the time most people were retiring for the night, Duan Xifeng became anxious. Finally she persuaded her mother to go out and make some inquiries. The woman asked around the village and discovered that Sun Wangquan had gone up the mountain with Zhao Qiaoying. Only this time they had gone without Egg Head. Xifeng's mother was a quick tempered woman with a wicked tongue. She never pretended to like her son-in-law, but she was forced to be civil to him for Xifeng and the baby's sake. The news that Wangquan and Qiaoying had gone up the mountain alone was enough to set her off. By the time she reached Qiaoying's home on the east side of the village, she had worked herself up into a towering rage. She planted herself in front of the gate, and bellowed for Wangquan to come out. When there was no response she unleashed her tongue on Qiaoying:

"Give me back our man, you vixen!" she shrilled. "You with your high-heeled shoes and your high and mighty 'age of the eighties' airs! You're just a man-stealing slut! There's never been anything as brazen in these Qinglong Mountains, even in the bad old days! Give me back our man, vixen, or I'll blacken you in this village! Vixen! Vixen! Vixen!"

Qiaoying's mother was just about to go out and look for her daughter when the commotion started. She knew all along that

Qiaoying was involved with Wangquan. All she prayed was that there be no scandal. So she quietly bolted her door and stayed in. Xifeng's mother stood outside and yelled till she was hoarse. But it was late, and without an audience to egg her on, she soon ran out of steam. Finally she went home, cursing all the way.

Next morning, Egg Head with his yellow army cap perched rakishly on his crusty scalp went around the village asking the young fellows whether they'd been harboring somebody's daughter the night before. The young women were joshed with an impudent question: "Did somebody's husband spend the night in your house?" Before long the village was buzzing like a hornet's nest.

As the morning wore on the families became really agitated. A search party was organized and fanned out across the mountains looking for the missing ones. By the time they found Wangquan and Qiaoying, it was past the noon hour. The searchers were puzzled how two people could have fallen into the Eighth Army's old cave and come through without a scratch.

"Was it comfy up there?" one fellow asked Wangquan impishly. "What did you do all night?"

"I slept," replied Wangquan, fixing the fellow with his wide, narrow eyes.

That put an end to further questions.

Wangquan and Qiaoying went to their homes, packed a few things in their knapsacks and left again. People in the street watched them go. No one tried to speak to them, for their expressions warded off any attempts at conversation. They watched them cross the stone bridge that led to the highway, and realized then what was happening. Sun Wanshui and Sun Fuchang were summoned, and they gave chase. They caught up with Wangquan and Qiaoying as they passed the old graveyard which marked the boundary of Old Well Village.

Two pairs of eyes glared at one another. No one knew what to say.

It was Sun Wanshui who broke the angry silence.

"What are you up to?"

"We're leaving," said Wangquan coldly. "It's obvious we can't go on living here. So we're leaving. What we'll do next, I don't know."

Sun Wanshui's straggly beard trembled. His eyes went from Qiaoying to his grandson and back again.

"What is this all about?" he pleaded. "Your father's gone, but you still have your grandfather, and your uncle Fuchang. There's nothing we can't discuss."

Wangquan turned away. "We were already man and wife when you forced us apart."

Sun Wanshui shuddered as if he'd been struck. His mouth twitched but no words came. Qiaoying held on to Wangquan's arm, fighting the tears that would not be held back.

"There's a time for everything, Wangquan," it was Sun Fuchang speaking in his usual flat-sounding voice that betrayed not a shred of emotion. "I speak now as the branch secretary of the village. There's to be a meeting this evening and it concerns you. You can leave in the morning."

Sun Wanshui stared at him blankly. Nothing made sense to him.

"Uncle, there's nothing to worry about," Sun Fuchang addressed the old man, but his eyes were on Wangquan and Qiaoying. "There's nothing to worry about for anyone."

A crowd gathered on the stone bridge. Everyone was craning their necks for a glimpse of what was happening. Qiaoying's glance went from the crowd to Sun Fuchang and finally rested on Wangquan. She ran her fingers through her wind-tossed hair.

"All right. We'll go back," she said firmly. "We're not afraid. If Wangquan has to go to jail, I'll wait for him."

She took Wangquan's arm, and slowly they walked towards the crowd on the bridge, their heads held high.

* * *

The word got around the village very quickly. By nightfall everyone knew there would be a party meeting that evening to settle the business between Sun Wangquan and Zhao Qiaoying.

As soon as the meeting began, Qiaoying put on her warm padded coat, tied a kerchief over her head, and went to the party offices. She did not go in but waited outside.

Duan Xifeng tried to stay home. She tried to keep her mind off the meeting with chores. But she was restless. In the end, she, too, went to the party offices. The two women waited in the bone crushing cold, trying not to notice each other, each wrapped in her separate solitude.

The meeting broke up at midnight. The two women rushed to meet him, as soon as Sun Wangquan left the building.

"Wangquan," Xifeng called out to him timidly, her heart in her throat.

He glanced at her coldly, as if she were a stranger and went quickly to Qiaoying. Xifeng looked around, and seeing a relative come out, caught him by the arm as he passed.

"How was it settled?" She covered her face and wept.

Wangquan took Qiaoying by the arm and steered her down the dark and quiet street without a backward glance.

They walked in silence. Qiaoying clutched Wangquan's arm tenderly. She recognized the grim look on his face and waited for him to speak. When he remained silent, she finally had to ask, "How was it settled?"

Still Wangquan remained silent.

"Tell me what happened," Qiaoying said, trying hard not to sound anxious. "We're in this together."

"They've recalled me from the well digging brigade, to replace Sun Fuchang as branch secretary."

Qiaoying's step faltered. Her eyes grew wide. For a moment she did not believe what she heard.

* * *

There was quite a hubbub over Sun Wangquan and Zhao Qiaoying before the meeting began. When Sun Fuchang called the meeting to order, he quickly put that topic out of reach, by announcing that the meeting had not been called to settle personal matters.

"The Duans have not pressed charges, so there is nothing to discuss," he said.

"This meeting has been called to discuss the matter of digging a well." He went on to inform the assemblage that the county brigade had released Sun Wangquan, at his request, and that the party branch of the commune had accepted Wangquan as his replacement when he stepped down. The only item of business on the agenda was to decide on the transfer of authority. After that announcement the meeting settled down to dull routine.

Sun Wangquan caused an uproar when he objected to being reassigned. Afterwards various people spoke. They recalled Wangquan's activities since he returned from the city after his graduation. They spoke in such glowing terms that the incident on Pancake Cliff became proof positive of Wangquan's dedication to finding water for Old Well Village. Finally, in spite of his objections, and upon the insistence of Sun Fuchang, Wangquan was unanimously elected branch secretary. Sun Fuchang would remain as his deputy, and would be responsible for the work of the secretary for the time being.

* * *

"Secretary! It's a ploy to keep you here," Qiaoying exclaimed angrily. The flame of hope that she would finally be with the man she loved, and break away from the constrictions of the village, flickered and died.

"What about us?" she asked dully.

"I'll do my best to leave."

"Leave," she spat the word. "You'll never leave. You have a home, a wife and a son. You'll never leave them. And to think of all the men in the world, I had to fall in love with you."

"Listen to me, Qiaoqiao," Wangquan tried to comfort her. "Sun Fuchang promised to let me go once the well is dug. I'm ninety percent sure we'll strike water this time. After that, we'll be free. But to leave now would be a pity."

"What about me? This is the second time you're leaving me, but you have no pity for me."

She took the packet of prunes she brought along for him, and threw them in his face.

Wangquan grabbed her by the wrist, and held her fast.

"Be reasonable," he pleaded. "The well is important to me. All right, it's an obsession. We've prayed for a well for generations. Why, you and I came close to losing our lives over it. When they started in on me with the well, I knew I had to stay. The well is my life. It's like a child."

His words trailed off into silence.

It was the word "child" that struck Qiaoying the hardest. She stamped her foot and burst into tears.

"What about my child?" she stormed. "You spineless creature.

You're not a man. You're a well ... I want my child. I want my child."

She tore herself free from him and ran down the street.

He did not try to stop her. Despair closed in on him.

He had not realized up to that moment, that aside from Qiaoying, he also loved his son. But all the love he had for those two could not replace his love for this patch of bone-dry earth and his well.

Forgive me, Qiaoqiao, he thought; forgive me.

* * *

Once more officialdom descended upon Old Well Village, drawn there by the discovery of the cave and its gruesome past. The bones of the fallen were given a decent burial. Many photographs were taken, and a history of the battle of Pancake Cliff and the secret munitions factory was written. A petition was made to preserve the area as it was, and the cave was placed under the jurisdiction of the Taihang Mountains Eighth Army Museum.

* * *

Three months went by. Work on the well was progressing as expected. The estimated depth of the well was about two hundred and fifty meters. But the brigade's machinery could not reach that depth. So the project was divided into two stages. The first stage was done by hand, and would go as far as the water table. The second stage would employ machinery to take the well deeper into the earth. The work brigade was made up of young men and women full of youthful enthusiasm and vitality, though the work was hard, and dangerous. As they dug deeper into the earth, the two-meter-wide opening of the well seemed to contract, until, looking up from the bottom, it resembled a lone star set in a night sky. One time a meter-high gasoline drum used for hoisting soil to the surface, broke its moorings and fell. The impact compressed it to a third of its height. The steel cable of the hoist constantly rubbing against the lighting cable gave off electric shocks. The experience prompted Egg Head to quip, "It's torture, but there's nothing you can do about it. Down here you take your chances. If the sides of the shaft give way, you're lost."

One night word got around that blind minstrels would be performing in the village. The young work crew was excited. No one wanted to work the night shift that day. Wangquan turned the problem over in his mind. The minstrels were probably the only ones they would have that year, so he declared a holiday.

Aside from the temple fairs, the blind minstrels were the only entertainment the mountain people had. Five or six blind men and women, carrying their bedrolls and instruments wandered from one village to the next. They moved along the mountain tracks caterpillar fashion, the left hand of one clamped tightly on the left shoulder of the person in front. Everywhere they went, the blind minstrels were greeted with great hilarity. The children were particularly excited, running out to meet them, and guiding them to their billet.

In a little while, the village elders came to meet the entertainers with gifts of tea and cigarettes. The bellows at kitchen fires began pumping, and soon the aroma of noodles, onion tops and garlic and spices danced in the air. This traditional hospitality of a small mountain village had not changed in a thousand years. These sightless wanderers brought joy to the simple mountain folk. They charmed the old with selections from heroic operas of the past; they quickened the pulse of young girls with their romantic mountain songs, and the children grew bug-eyed at their acrobatics. But the minstrels' magic worked only in the mountains. On the city streets they would be despised as one more band of beggars. In the village they were spared the humiliation of straining to hear the coins falling on the hard ground. Here they sat in comfort on fresh mats, smoking good cigarettes and accepting polite offers of money.

Lights were strung up around the stage in front of the Dragon King's Temple, and a crowd gathered long before the performance was to start. An old blind man with oozing eye sockets opened the proceedings with "Ten Verses on the Policy of Responsibility," and followed it up with a ditty called "One is Best." These topical items, treated with irreverent slang, broke the ice. In the midst of the applause, a blind youth with the broad shoulders of an athlete took the stage.

He felt around the little table that stood in the center of the stage, and found a packet of cigarettes and matches. He lit two cigarettes, and sticking one in each nostril, played a tune on his horn. It was a popular tune called "A Hundred Birds Greet the Phoenix." With every breath he took, the cigarettes protruding from the young musician's nostrils flared, and puffs of smoke billowed from the bell of his horn. The audience applauded wildly. Next, the youth took a carrot from his pocket, and proceeded to munch it while he played his next selection, a tune called "The Lanterns." He finished the carrot at the same time as the tune ended.

The children were particularly captivated by the performance, hooting and clapping. The young people who had other things on their minds, shifted about nervously.

Wangquan stood beside Xifeng. He could see Qiaoying alone in the distance, standing in the half light, and his heart contracted painfully. Xifeng, who seldom appeared in public with Wangquan and her children, glanced at her man out of the corner of her eye and smiled. She was content.

A while later, Wangquan looked again, but Qiaoying was gone. His eyes searched the crowd, but she had quietly slipped away. He recalled how they had met in this very place, two springs ago. There was a performance that night too. But they were free and happy then. Suddenly the performance paled. He could not bear to watch the antics on the stage a moment longer. To Xifeng he made an excuse that he was tired, and was going home.

Xifeng did not object, but thrust the baby into his arms.

"The baby's tired too," she said simply, but in her heart she knew the child was her strongest weapon against Qiaoying.

The street was empty. No lover awaited him. Love was gone, leaving him desolate. The night was still. Not a breath of wind stirred. Even the dogs were quiet. Wangquan pressed the child's tender cheek against his, and found a little comfort as he wended his way home.

Meanwhile the performance was reaching a noisy climax. The only woman in the troupe had sung seven or eight numbers but the crowd would not let her leave the stage.

Egg Head and his cronies kept shouting, "Give us a real song! We want a juicy one!"

The woman was not pretty, but she had a nice smile. She

smiled now, and clearing her throat launched into a bawdy song about illicit love.

"No! No! No!" the youngsters yelled even as she sang, "You'll have to do better than that!"

The singer faltered and stopped. The old fiddler got to his feet, and bowing to the audience said, smiling, "Friends and comrades, we aim to please. But I regret we cannot comply with your request. Not because we don't want to, but because we don't dare. The Chairman and the party have taught us to cultivate loftier thoughts."

Some sixth sense told the old secretary Sun Fuchang that trouble was brewing. So he got up and left. The women whispered nervously to one another and started leaving in threes and fours.

The old blind fiddler was still trying to calm the audience that was threatening to turn ugly. "Wherever we go, we do our best to follow the leadership of the party. But if the Secretary of the village would issue a directive."

"The secretary?" hooted Egg Head, "Both secretaries have gone home!"

The fiddler recognized the voice as that of the young man who had gone out of his way to help draw in the crowds.

"Who are you, young sir?" he asked.

"He's the secretary's son," shouted Xizhu and some of the other youths.

"He's a failed scholar, but our next secretary!"

The old man nodded, dabbed his wet eye sockets with his coat sleeve, and sawed out the opening bars of a song called "Picking Bean Sprouts."

The singer smiled faintly and trying to pull a long face, sang out:

> July is July,
> August is August,
> Out gathering bean sprouts with a basket
> Oh, dear mother!

It was a popular bawdy song which everybody knew. Every verse ended with "Oh, dear mother." The young audience joined in noisily when it came round to that line. The merriment was infectious, for even the musicians were laughing now. Only the woman managed to keep a straight face, singing:

That stupid youth
Was unreasonable,
He dragged me into the sorghum field
O, dear mother . . .

"What did you do in the sorghum field?" hooted Xizhu, amid general laughter.

"Quiet everybody," shouted Egg Head, "we're getting to the nitty-gritty of it!"

The lyrics got more and more bawdy. Finally, the blind singer was reduced to humming the really raunchy parts. But the audience knew the words, and happily filled in for her.

It was well after midnight when the performance was finally over.

* * *

The next day Egg Head did not report for work.

On the morning of the third day, when Egg Head appeared on the well site, Xizhu was the first to tease him, asking whether the blind woman had exhausted him.

"Get out of here," said Egg Head, giving Xizhu a shove. "Only a stinking bedbug like you gets flattened with one squeeze. Outside of arms and legs, there's not an inch of you that's stiff."

The young men laughed, and the girls muttered, "Filthy devil."

"Filthy devil is it?" Egg Head turned on the girls. "I wouldn't dream of putting a finger on you!"

"You're queer, you know," pronounced Xizhu. "What do you do with the bras and panties you steal off the girls' laundry line?"

"That's a lie!" cried Egg Head, turning pale.

"Like hell it's a lie. I bet you're wearing a bra right now!" yelled Xizhu. "Why don't you show us, if you've got the guts."

Egg Head leaped on Xizhu, and the two tumbled on the ground, kicking and punching. The girls also leaped into the fray and pinned Egg Head down. There was a mad scuffle, then Xizhu jumped to his feet, triumphantly bearing aloft a pale green brassiere.

"What did I tell you!" he crowed.

Everybody laughed. Egg Head staggered to his feet, adjusted his yellow army cap on his scabby head and glared at his tormentors.

"You bunch of ingrates," he sneered. "You don't know how well off you are, having Master Sun for a friend. So now you're suddenly prim and proper, a bunch of virgins!"

The girls closed ranks around him. Good natured teasing suddenly turned into anger.

"Enough nonsense," Sun Wangquan's voice brought them up short. Wangquan snatched the pale green brassiere the boys were gleefully tossing back and forth and threw it on the bonfire.

"Get to work," he shouted. The crowd slowly dispersed. Only Zhao Qiaoying and Sun Wangquan had not taken part in the commotion. Wangquan watched the flames consume the brassiere, anger flaring when he noticed the embarrassed look on Qiaoying's face. He followed Egg Head down the well. As soon as he stepped out of the hoist, Wangquan collared Egg Head and delivered a stinging blow to the face. Egg Head staggered backwards, squealing in surprise.

"What did you do that for?"

"Who have you been stealing from?" demanded Wangquan. Another blow smashed into Egg Head, sending him reeling.

"So, I lust after a woman," cried Egg Head. "Does that give you the right to hit me?"

The next blow plastered Egg Head against the side of the well.

Egg Head crumpled in a heap and he began to blubber, "You've got two women dangling on a string. You can sleep with whichever you fancy. But I've never even sniffed a woman. Go ahead and kill me. You'd be putting me out of my misery."

Sun Wangquan was embarrassed by Egghead's bawling. He seized a shovel and began digging furiously.

Toward the end of the shift, while Zhao Qiaoying was running the hoist that was lifting a heavy load of earth and rock to the surface, the rope suddenly slipped off the pulley. At the same time the brake on the winch failed. Qiaoying seized the rope and yelled for help. In a flash the hugh weight was plummeting down the well pulling her along with it. She felt herself falling. A rush of air knocked the breath out of her. She was losing consciousness.

For a split second she thought of Wangquan at the bottom of the well. There was a moment of euphoria as she plunged downward. She struggled to cry out his name, to tell him one last time that she loved him, before darkness swallowed her.

The falling hoist missed Wangquan by a hair's breadth, but Egg Head was killed instantly, and Qiaoying's leg was broken.

Once more the peace and quiet of Old Well Village was shattered by tragedy.

While Sun Wangcai's family prepared to bury their dead, Wangquan, with the help of Xizhu and the other youths, made a crude stretcher and drove Qiaoying to the county hospital on a tractor.

The village gossips were soon at work. It was rumored that Qiaoying had been dragged down the well in an effort to save Wangquan. Indeed, Wangquan stayed at the hospital with Qiaoying for two days, and gave blood twice. This simple act of compassion took on a new significance. Now that the blood of the lovers was mingled, it was asked, who was to keep them apart? For once Xifeng's mother was silent, and kept to her house.

On the day of Egg Head's funeral, Secretary Li of the County Party Committee returned to the village. That day, Wangquan left the hospital and hitching a ride on his jeep, went back to Old Well in a daze to bid his friend farewell.

A solemn group of friends, relatives and officials clustered around the open coffin. Egg Head was laid out with his head swathed in bandages, so that only his bulbous nose and mouth showed. A new yellow army cap was on his head. His favorite deck of cards was placed beside his hand, together with two packets of filter-tipped Phoenix brand cigarettes and his lighter. A fountain pen and a ballpoint pen protruded from the breast pocket of his jacket. Someone had pinned a university badge on his chest. There was also a neat pile of magazines full of pictures of pretty film actresses, and on his wrist was the almost-new watch he treasured.

Just then a car from the public security office drove up. The strangers had asked their way to Sun Fuchang's house and blundered into a funeral. Secretary Li drew the men aside and asked their business. At first the strangers were reluctant to state their errand, but after some probing the story gradually came out.

The Department of Culture heard that a troupe of blind minstrels had given a bawdy performance in the village, and decided to make a public example of their folly. The Public Security Office was alerted and an investigation began. The minstrels were rounded up and questioned, and it was discovered that the blind woman had slept with Egg Head in exchange for four yuan and five catties worth of grain coupons. When the woman was told by the other women held in custody with her that it would go badly for her if she admitted accepting payment, she quickly changed her tune. The next time she was questioned, the woman insisted that she had been raped. A serious charge had been made, and the Public Security Office had come to arrest Egg Head.

Sun Wangquan stood beside Secretary Li and listened to this whispered exchange numb with grief. Sun Wangcai, his school friend—work mate—prankster—the happy-go-lucky Egg Head was gone forever, his brief unfulfilled life snuffed out.

The lid of the coffin was hammered into place. Sun Fuchang stood impassive as a pillar of stone. His wife groveled in the dust keening.

* * *

After the funeral the village sank into lethargy. Work on the well came to a standstill. It was whispered around the village that the diggers had disturbed the Dragon King and he had vented his anger on the trespassers. They reminded one another that in the old days, a necromancer had to be consulted before a well was dug. This was clearly an unlucky cistern, and more lives would be lost if work continued. It did not take long for Wangquan and Sun Fuchang to discover that the village sorceress, Third Auntie, was at the bottom of all the superstitious talk. She was immediately brought to the village administration. Third Auntie's fat cheeks trembled with fear. Sun Fuchang was in a towering rage. He pounded his desk and threatened to have her sent up to the County Security Office.

"However," he continued more calmly, seeing that the woman was completely cowed, "since you say the Dragon King forbids the well to be dug, tonight you will go and ask his permission."

The sorceress searched the old secretary's face warily, but Sun Fuchang's face was a blank.

"You know how to manage these things," he said in his flat voice, giving Wangquan a meaningful look. "Tonight you will make things right."

At dusk, the Third Auntie put incense, little buns, eggs, a tin of pork, and good white sorghum wine in a basket and waddled up to Pine Creek where the well was. A swarm of children and curious youths followed her.

The sorceress laid out the offerings on the northwest side of the well. Then she lit the incense and kneeling, touched her head to the ground, muttering incantations. Finally she struggled to her feet, and poured the wine down the well. The ritual completed, the Third Auntie toddled home. But before she reached her door some mysterious power seemed to take possession of her. Her body went rigid and her eyes rolled back in their sockets till they almost disappeared. A tremor rippled through her, and her limbs jerked about in a grotesque dance. She whirled about faster and faster, until her breath became a noisy gurgle. Her legs became rubbery. She wobbled and fell. For a moment she lay on the ground, a great heap of trembling flesh. Slowly she came to.

"The Dragon King has been appeased," she pronounced wearily. "He's given permission to sink the well, and promised there will be water." Suddenly a strange look came into her protruding eyes, and in a half strangled voice she cried out, "The Dragon King drank a whole bottle of good sorghum wine." She looked so wild and dishevelled that the onlookers backed away from her.

The sorceress' antics silenced the grumbling of the women and the old folk.

That same night a meeting was called, and a resolution was passed to finish the well. Nevertheless, the brigade seemed to have lost heart. Next morning a crowd gathered round the well. Wangquan and Sun Fuchang took the first shift.

The fetid air, laced with the smell of death, and the blood-stained earth was more than Sun Fuchang could bear. He leaned against the side of the well, lit a cigarette and inhaled savagely. His face was as expressionless as ever, but the cigarette trembled ever so slightly between his lips.

Sun Wangquan shoveled the patches of blood onto the hoist, and as it slowly rose to the surface Sun Fuchang's knees buckled. The fingers of his broad, calloused hands clawed at the earth, and silently, he wept.

As the blood soaked soil reached the surface, Xizhu, Sanze and the other youths gathered there, fell silent. A few had tears in their eyes.

The mad old man, Sun Wanshan suddenly appeared out of nowhere. A filthy rag was wound round his head turban fashion. The padding in his clothes had shifted, bunching along the seams, giving him a curiously lumpy appearance. He took in the solemn faces around him, and a fleeting moment of understanding darted through his mind. But before he could grasp it, it was gone again. Sun Wanshui pounced on him and started to drag him away.

"Did someone get killed? Always digging wells, digging wells," the madman gibbered and clapped his hands.

Sun Wanshui tightened his grip on his mad brother, but he could not keep him quiet.

"It's a curse!" shouted Wanshan. "The mountain's hurting! No wonder it curses you!"

The mist was rising. The peaks of Qinglong Mountain were etched against the lighting sky, but the river and the village were still shrouded in deep blue shadows. The wind whispered through the stillness of the dawn. The mountain reared skyward, mysterious and remote, clutching its secrets to itself.

Chapter 10

The bare mountains and the barren earth and dusty humanity staggered into the drought ridden spring of 1983. A few hardy sprouts pushed their way out of the soil. The parched fields showed a hint of green, but it did not last. The sun blazed down, and the tender shoots withered. Nothing grew on the mountainsides. Dogs slinked around with their tongues lolling. Scrawny chickens flapped their wings. Even the lizards kept to the shade, gasping for breath. Carrying poles, carts, jeeps, tractors and trains were pressed into transporting water. But the shortage was severe and no simple solution was at hand.

In the city, schools and factories closed. The hotels and guest houses were shuttered. The hospital stopped admitting patients.

In the mountains, cattle were being driven great distances to the neighboring counties where there was water. The road leading to Old Well Village was clogged with herds of cows, goats, horses and mules. They plodded along, heads drooping. Not a mane quivered nor a tail swished. The long procession went by and the dust it stirred up hung in the air like a grayish yellow screen.

Work continued on the deep well at Pine Creek. But the people were beginning to lose heart, and there were doubts whether they would strike water at all. The old folks were gathering in little knots and whispering together. One day, Sun Wanshui and a few of his cronies marched up to the village administration office to see the assistant secretary, Sun Fuchang. After cigarettes had been passed around and pleasantries exchanged, Sun Wanshui came straight to the point. The old folks decided that it was time to seek divine intervention to end the drought.

Sun Fuchang chuckled, "Uncle Wanshui, that's a superstition carried over from feudal times. The authorities wouldn't allow it."

Wanshui hastened to explain that they did not suggest holding a procession of the Dragon King as in the old days.

"All we need is a tractor to go into town and bring back an opera troupe, and offer the Dragon King a few performances."

"And you think a few performances would do the trick?" said Sun Fuchang incredulously. "But the unit doesn't have the money to pay the actors.

The old folks had already thought of that. They proposed that money be collected from the villagers according to the amount of land they held and the size of the family, just as it was in the days of the cooperative.

So you think you've outsmarted me, old coffin-stuffers, Sun Fuchang thought to himself. As it happened, the proposal was no news to him. He had been told. What did take him by surprise was that the unit would not be responsible financially, nor would it involve him personally. Sun Fuchang was reluctant to interfere with the plans out of deference to Sun Wanshui, who had a unique position in the village. Wanshui's brother Wanjin had gone south with the army after liberation and settled in Sichuan province. Now he was an important cadre in Chengdu and even the County Secretary had to bow to his wishes. Aside from that, Sun Wanshui was the oldest member of the Sun clan, which put him a notch higher on the social ladder than Sun Fuchang. Moreover the people needed spiritual comfort and Sun Fuchang could see no harm in it, provided they did not break any rules, and did not involve him personally. Another consideration lurked at the back of his mind. Money was required if the work on the well at Pine Creek was to continue. The present situation would set a precedent for the time when the villagers would be asked to contribute toward the completion of the well.

Sun Fuchang smiled amiably at Wanshui, and said, "You want

to put on a performance and I want to dig a well. What if we come up against an obstacle? What'll we do?"

The old men looked at one another, not quite grasping the secretary's meaning.

"The performances and the well are two different things," Wanshui replied, "Silly as we may be, we accept that."

Sun Fuchang slapped his thigh, as if some momentous decision had been reached. "You can have your performances, but there are conditions. No one must be forced to contribute. I will tell you right now, my family will not contribute. As for using the tractor, you have to talk to the driver, Sanze. That's his responsibility. Whichever way you look at it, you're catering to superstition. If there is trouble afterwards, you're on your own."

The old men agreed heartily, and after a few more pleasantries they left, contented.

A few days later Sun Wanshui and the sorceress Third Auntie rode the tractor into the city to engage the players.

As the actors were unloading gear beside the bridge leading into the village, a tractor with the markings of the Zhejiang Province Construction brigade roared past carrying the carcasses of a pig and a goat.

The sorceress Third Auntie poked Sun Wanshui in the ribs, and whispered, "What did I tell you, they're going up to Red Dragon Grotto."

A bridge was being built across the Qinglong River five li downstream from the village. A construction brigade was moved in from Zhejiang Province to do the job. This was a group of lean and tough looking young men and women who were brought in for their hardiness. The spring rains failed, and the river was dry, so work on the bridge was progressing at a fast clip. Then the villagers in the area began surreptitiously praying for rain. The workers on the bridge were worried that heavy rains might cause flash floods which would hamper their progress, so they were taking blood offerings to the Red Dragon Grotto and praying that the drought would continue.

Wanshui glanced at the tractor as it disappeared in a cloud of dust, and the actors wrestling their gear into the village and muttered complacently, "People have always prayed for rain. But nobody has ever prayed for drought."

In the old days when a play was given in a temple, the first performance was dedicated to the gods. The Dragon King's statue was placed in front of the stage, and he alone watched the performance. But the Dragon King's statue was destroyed and a live audience clustered around the stage from the first night. Although it was supposed to be a religious ritual, the performance was no different than any other.

Before the play began, three actors strode onto the stage. Each recited a few lines of verse, vaguely expressing humanity's yearning for the blessings of the gods. At the end of each stanza the actor would fold his hands and bow in the direction of the temple. After each actor had recited his lines, all three joined in reciting the final stanza in unison. Then the performance began.

A light breeze came up as the play ended the first night. The moon and stars were half hidden by a thin veil of cloud. And the people said to one another, "The weather is changing. Perhaps the gods do exist after all."

On the second night great black clouds boiled over the southeastern horizon, and the air felt dense with rain. Wanshui hobbled backstage delightedly passing around cigarettes and telling whoever would listen that faith could move mountains. He promised the actors a bonus if it rained. That night the actors leaped and roared about the stage for all they were worth, and the audience clapped and shouted their approval. Suddenly there was a gust of wind, and lightning ripped the sky. Thunder rumbled and the darkness deepened. There were a few spatters of rain and the clouds moved on.

The following night there was another performance, but nothing happened. The disappointed villagers began to grumble, saying that the workers from Zhejiang had turned the gods against them with their blood offerings. Sun Wanshui stalked home angrily, muttering to himself. In these hard times, even the gods were taking bribes. He shook his head, mumbling over and over, "I don't understand, I don't understand."

* * *

The day the canopy was put in place over the well, Sun Wanshui carried a huge red flag up to the well site, and told Wangquan to fly it over the well. Wangquan understood that his grandfather meant it as a talisman to ward off evil. But red was the color of joy as well, thus the flag could be symbol of joy. It was merely a matter of point of view.

A few days after the red flag was hoisted, the county well digging brigade telephoned Sun Wangquan. Geologist Sun was giving a week-long seminar on water resources and he was invited to attend. Wangquan felt he could be spared for that length of time, and went off to the city. After he was registered, Wangquan bought a box of biscuits and went to visit Qiaoying, who was convalescing in the hospital. A stronger bond of life and death linked them now. The preciousness of life and love outweighed all other considerations.

After the evening meal, Wangquan and the geologist were strolling in the gardens of the guest house when Qiaoying appeared unannounced. She was pert and pretty, quite herself again. Actually Qiaoying was fully recovered, but the doctors chose to keep her in the hospital a few days longer for observation. She called Wangquan's name and waved. Wangquan hurried to her side and quickly guided her out of the gate, not slowing down till they were clear of the guest house and curious eyes.

"Where do you want to go?" he asked blushing, and a little annoyed.

Qiaoying looked at him standing tall and straight beside her. He was trim and handsome in his clean blue work suit. She was happy as a child on a holiday.

"Let's go to the station," she suggested. "The train from Beijing will be in soon. I like to watch the people."

"Watch people?"

"I often go to the station just to watch the people arriving from Beijing and Taiyuan. It's more fun than watching television." When no one was looking she grabbed his hand and held it.

The express from Beijing was just pulling in. In a moment the platform was thronged with people carrying suitcases and parcels. Qiaoying's eyes darted excitedly in and out of the crowd.

"There's a clothes peddler," she remarked, curling her lip as a middle-aged man lumbered past dragging a heavy bag made of red and blue striped vinyl. Next, a young couple carrying a suitcase with stickers of Beijing plastered all over it caught her eye. They also had boxes of cakes and dates from Beijing, a bunch of plastic flowers, and a statue made of plaster of Paris.

"They were on their honeymoon" Qiaoying tried to sound matter-of-fact but she could not keep the longing out of her voice. Wangquan turned away pretending to be interested in something else. But the people who really interested Qiaoying were the natives of Beijing who had been assigned jobs in the city. They came with all their worldly goods strapped on carts. Fourteen-inch color television sets, stereo sound systems, a birthday cake, bundles of fine vermicelli, an electric rice cooker, and jars of Beijing pickles. Qiaoying stared at a young couple in their thirties. The man was wearing a light brown leather jacket, pushing the cart. The woman had on a pair of high-heeled shoes, and a pair of fine gray slacks that hugged her waist and buttocks. She held onto a boy of about five or six, a trim replica of herself.

Qiaoying watched the trio disappear into the crowds, and she drooped against Wangquan's shoulder.

"Will we ever have a life like theirs?" she wondered. "That man was not as tall or good-looking as you. And the woman had a face full of pimples. But they have a better life than we do. When I'm lonely, I come to the station and look at the people. I try to picture their lives; what they eat and drink; what they think about; where they work; what gives them pleasure; where they sleep. Sometimes I get so depressed I want to find a place where I can howl like a wolf."

Wangquan smiled. "You think too much. Why envy others? As they say, 'someone else's pasture is always greener.' There are city folks who envy us."

"Not envying others is not being noble. It's the Ah Q mentality manifesting itself. City folk come out to the country, and gnaw a couple ears of corn, and half a cucumber. It's a break in their routine, and it's fun. They don't do it because life in the country suits them."

Wangquan could not rebut that.

It was getting late, but Qiaoying was not ready to leave. "Stay with me a while longer," she pleaded. "I miss you so much ... and we have so little time."

Wangquan let himself be steered into the waiting room. They sat on the long bench, arms around each other whispering all the secret things locked in their hearts. When Wangquan glanced at Qiaoying's watch some time later it was past midnight.

"The guest house locks its door at eleven o'clock. I've been locked out."

"It's all right," Qiaoying chuckled, "I didn't plan on letting you leave me alone in the hospital. We'll spend the night here. It's warm and dry and a lot nicer than Pancake Cliff."

Wangquan had planned to learn all he could from Geologist Sun, but his week in the city had gotten off to a bad start. On the first day he was not only absent without leave, he had also broken discipline. But he was also deeply moved by Qiaoying. In any case he would not be let into the guest house. They snuggled close, whispering until they grew drowsy. Their lips met in a surreptitious kiss that set their pulses racing. They screwed their eyes shut and tried to sleep. But the harder they tried, the more wakeful they became. Scattered moments of their night on Pancake Cliff whirled through their minds.

It was the most cliched question that lovers ever ask each other, but Qiaoying asked it, as if it were uniquely hers: "Why do you love me?"

Wangquan mulled the question over, and answered with a mischievous grin, "I love you because you're a good worker!"

"Be serious."

"On the other hand, it may be because you have pretty eyes."

"Anything else?"

"Yes. But I'd rather not say."

"Whisper in my ear."

"Hey, you, get up! Get up!" Suddenly a tall policeman with a nose like the beak of a hawk loomed over them. "Show me your tickets!"

Qiaoying straightened up and ran her fingers through her hair.

"We're just sitting here. We're not going anywhere."

"You want to spend the night, find a hotel. This is a waiting room."

Qiaoying looked around. "Why are you picking on us?" she demanded.

The policeman pointed his chin at the door, "Who's picking on you? They're all gone."

A few farmers who had settled down on their luggage for the

night were straggling out the door with their children trailing behind.

The sight of the farmers meekly wandering into the night angered Qiaoying. "Why are you picking on farmers?" she demanded angrily.

The policeman looked down his long nose at her.

"I can pick on whoever I feel like. Peasants are all alike. With a little cash in their pockets, they think they can fly. And you can take your objections to the vice chairman if you want."

Qiaoying got to her feet, gave the policeman a devastating look and stalked out of the room.

"Why get so het up?" said Wangquan once they were outside. "He could see we had no luggage. That's why he asked."

"It's not that!" Qiaoying was still angry, and Wangquan caught the brunt of it.

"It's the way you look!"

Wangquan looked at himself. In the greenish glow of the street lamps, his wrinkled blue suit looked shabby indeed. But his suede shoes were nice. He thought he looked quite presentable. Now he wasn't sure.

"I look plain, but you needn't be ashamed of me," he said.

"You're a fool, Wangquan. Only the rich can afford to look plain. For the likes of you, plain means 'poor.' "

"There's nothing wrong with being plain," muttered Wangquan, though he felt a sting of truth in what Qiaoying said.

Another train was pulling in. The public address system crackled to life, calling on travelers to have their tickets ready for boarding.

Qiaoying watched people streaming through the gate toward the train.

"It's the train to Beijing. I wonder what it's like, how people live. Here, a boy starts earning money in his teens, to build a house and find a wife. The dumb ones stay single or they have an arrangement. The smart ones who marry are soon stuck with a child. Then they have to earn more money so that when the child grows up he'll have a nest egg to build a house and marry. Finally, when that's all behind him, he still has to earn enough money for a decent burial. Life is a cycle of drudgery."

"That's the way it is, but it doesn't have to stay that way," Wangquan tried to reason with her. "It's up to us to change things. For instance if our well is a success, it could change many things."

"I don't care," Qiaoying cut him short. "I'm getting on that train right now. Are you coming?"

"I can't do that. Maybe after the seminar."

"We'll go after the seminar, if you really mean it."

"There's also the well. We've reached a critical stage."

"You're tied hand and foot, to the land, to the crops, and to the well. And don't forget your wife and child!"

She turned and walked away quickly. The train was about to leave. Qiaoying walked past the ticket taker, her head held high, the heels of her high-heeled shoes clicking smartly on the cement. Wangquan tried to follow but he was stopped at the gate, because he looked like a peasant and had no ticket. The warning bell sounded. The conductor stood on the steps and held the door for Qiaoying. No matter how he pleaded, the ticket taker shut the gate in Wangquan's face. Wangquan stuck his hand through the bars, grasped the latch and twisted with all his might. There was a tearing sound. The latch gave way and the gate flew open. The terrified ticket taker rushed off, not waiting to see what would happen next. The train was already moving. Wangquan barely had time to toss his wallet through the window for Qiaoying. In it were twenty yuan and Shanxi province ration coupons for ten catties of grain.

"Qiaoqiao, get off at the next station and come back!"

Qiaoying took no notice of him.

The next day Wangquan went to the hospital and made excuses for Qiaoying with the doctor, so her absence wouldn't be reported to public security. From then on he spent the days in the classroom, and the evenings copying Geologist Sun's *Basic Geology,* which was out of print. His days were so full that there was no time to be lonely. Still there were spare moments when he missed Qiaoying and worried how she fared in far off Beijing.

* * *

When the seminar was over, there was still no sign of Qiaoying. Wangquan was anxious to get back to the well and start drilling, so he went home.

He was examining some stone samples the following noon, when he heard a woman singing in the distance. He recognized the teasing love song, and the voice of the singer at once. He peered into the distance, his heart hammering. Far as she was, he recognized the woman's walk. It was Qiaoying going down to the river.

Wangquan took a roundabout route. When he came to the river bank she was waiting.

"I missed you," she said reddening. "It's no fun being alone."

He knew what it was like to be alone, and he was still a little sore. "What took you so long?"

"Look." She shook a handful of seed from a little cloth bag and smiled proudly. "These are superior grade corn seeds. I brought back other seeds too, and some chemicals."

She had met some agricultural experts and professors in Beijing who were impressed with her knowledge. The upshot was that she was given sample seeds and chemicals, and told that she would be welcome to visit again. They dubbed her "agricultural technician." Beijing gave Qiaoying a taste of city life she would not forget. She thought she was a smart dresser; now she saw herself as a parody of the real thing. She was dazzled by the billboards, jostled by the crowds on Wangfujing, and Qianmen and the Forbidden City. She rubbed shoulders with foreigners. The streets were so wide she thought she would never get from one side to the other. Once she dropped a handkerchief on the ground, and when she picked it up there wasn't a speck of dust on it. It took her days to discover that the streets were washed every night. The boulevards were covered with flowers and greenery all protected by wrought iron fences and kept neater than any garden patch she'd ever seen. There were streets, and shoes, and clothes, and more streets. And everywhere there were people. Men looking at women. Women looking at men. The very pavement pulsed with life.

"I think of those streets and I want to cry. These mountains are suffocating me!"

Listening to her, Wangquan trembled inside. What is to become of us, he thought. Still, a stubborn faith in the future burned in him.

"Beijing was built by man. Once we strike water, life will be easier. Some day, life in these Taihang Mountains will be just as good. Just you wait and see."

"By then we'll all be in our graves."

Xizhu came by leading his horse and a mule, and carrying a plough.

"What secrets are you two whispering?" Xizhu was in a playful mood. "Speak up and let's hear it."

Wangquan was not in the mood for joking: "What shall we do, Qiaoying? Find a stone wall and bash our heads in and die?"

Qiaoying ignored him, and turning to Xizhu said airily, "Don't just stand there, we've got work to do."

Xizhu hitched the plough to the animals, Wangquan mixed phosphates with manure for fertilizer and Qiaoying scattered the seeds.

It was only a small plot of land, about the size of a postage stamp, situated on the river's edge. As they worked, Qiaoying noticed that under the parched surface the soil was damp.

"That was Wangquan's doing," remarked Xizhu as he guided the plough. "When you were in the hospital, he would come here every day, cut ice from the river and bury it in the ground."

This ancient method of conserving moisture in the soil had fallen into disuse. It was strenuous work and time consuming. Only a man such as Wangquan would do it. She watched him, silently following the plough, spreading the fertilizer. He was like a rock; hard and silent but strong. And she was like a brook babbling on without purpose. She needed a steadying influence. She needed him. She murmured a prayer that the gods might show them a way.

Wangquan worked silently. Cutting and burying ice was hard work, but it was worth it. Last year Qiaoying had a good crop of cotton and peanuts using her scientific methods. Wangquan hoped that if he could help her with this crop the earth would keep her in the village, and somehow they would find a way to be together.

The field was soon planted. Qiaoying stretched strips of plastic over the furrows to protect the soil from the broiling sun, and to conserve moisture. The dry wind stirred the soil and covered them with a film of yellow dust. At dusk the work was done. Xizhu unhitched his animals and went on home. Left alone, Wangquan took a handkerchief and gently dabbed the sweat from Qiaoying's face.

"You must be tired, after all the running about in Beijing and being fresh out of the hospital."

Qiaoying smiled wearily. She started to say that she had fun in Beijing when a little fox ambled out of some bushes by the river.

Qiaoying tiptoed towards it, speaking to it softly, calling it pet and friend. The little fox cocked its head at her, its long bushy tail wagging, on the alert. But it would not let Qiaoying get too close. It dove into the underbrush and scurried away.

"Maybe I'm not a fox fairy after all," Qiaoying remarked.

"It knows you've been to the big city," Wangquan teased.

Once more she began to tell Wangquan about Beijing. Actually she did not see as much of the city as she claimed. She was hoping that some day they would go there together. She dreamed of walking down the street with him, arm in arm. It was a secret she would tell no one. For she knew it was nothing but a dream. So she smiled and chatted gaily. High above them the mountains were fading into the bluish green twilight.

Chapter 11

Dusk.

A breeze wandering through the valley of the Qinglong River scattered the column of smoke rising from the kitchen fires of Old Well Village, worrying it into layer upon layer of blue-gray haze. The rains of early summer turned the mountainside a tender shade of green that glimmered through the growing darkness.

As daylight faded, the sound of a gong rang through the village. Somewhere a voice hoarse from shouting announced that a meeting was called after the evening meal. Actually there was a public address system in the village, but it had broken down. For the last two years the gong was still the most reliable harbinger of change. The distribution of land, cattle and farm implements were all ushered in by the gong. Now it rang out once more.

When the evening meal was over, the heads of each household made their way to the Dragon King's Temple, some with cigarettes dangling between their lips, and others clutching their sewing.

On the stage in the temple courtyard stood a black lacquered coffin. At the foot of the stage was an ancient, five-foot tall stone tablet that once stood before the main hall of the Goddess Temple. The front and back of the tablet had been worn smooth. But the decorations around the edges and the four characters at the top that meant "Eternal Honor" had been carefully restored. The same table that had been used the night the blind minstrels played was placed in front of the stage. A lamp with a long extension cord stood on it. In its glow sat the secretary Sun Wangquan, the assistant secretary Sun Fuchang, and the old man Sun Wanshui. When everyone was assembled, Sun Fuchang stood, pounded the table and called the meeting to order.

Sun Fuchang came to the point at once.

"This is a meeting of the village people, chaired by our Uncle Wanshui, and it concerns our new well. You all know the county contributed five thousand yuan, and the unit put up thirteen thousand more for its construction. But we need more money to take the well down to its proper depths. The cadres have studied the problem of raising money, and we've concluded that the only solution is to sell the willow trees along the river. All the livestock and the farm implements have been distributed, and Sanze has leased the tractor. We have nothing to sell and nothing to pawn. What shall we do?"

Although people whispered to one another, no one spoke up. The courtyard buzzed like a nest of disturbed hornets.

Sun Wanshui got to his feet next. He stroked his scraggly beard, and cleared his throat and waited for the hum of voices to die down.

"I'll say this much," he began. "When the spring rains failed, it was my idea to put on the ritual plays, and I went to you for money. I was asking you to take a chance. But this time I am asking you to bet on a sure thing. In the thousand years since our ancestors came here from Niuwang Fort in Hebei this land has supported us. It has not been an easy life. They say cattle die of thirst here; we break our backs working here, and women won't marry our men. Our young men stay single, or have arrangements. Brothers share a woman. These things are a disgrace. Out of the big clans—the Suns, the Duans, the Zhaos, and the Lis—no less than sixteen men gave their lives digging wells. Countless others were injured. My father died praying for rain; my brother went mad; not long ago my son was killed. Why do we give our bodies so freely, but cling to our cash? I am counting the days till I lie in the old graveyard. But I still have a dream; a dream that we finally strike water, so the ones who went before will not have died in vain. I have nothing to give except this coffin, for what it's worth. As long as we strike water, it matters not how I am buried."

"What if there's no water," a voice shouted from the crowd, "then we'd be throwing our hard-earned cash down the pit!"

Sun Fuchang spoke again: "We've thrown money down dry pits before. The dry holes all over Qinglong Mountain are proof. But this is the first well we've sunk scientifically. Wangquan has studied these mountains from Shanxi to Hebei and back again. And he almost lost his life on Pancake Cliff. I pledge one hundred yuan in the name of my son Wangcai."

Mention of the dead youth silenced the crowd momentarily.

"Since Wangquan has all the answers, let's hear from him," another shouted.

"What can I say," responded Wangquan. "I know there's water down there, but we need money to reach it."

"We will not be cheated by one of our own," Sun Wanshui spoke again, and pointing at the stone table, continued, "I had my grandson smooth out that tablet. I propose that the names of the donors, and the amounts they gave be recorded on the back of the tablet. When we strike water, that event will be recorded on the face of the tablet so that generations from now people will remember how we overcame our hardships."

But the doubters persisted.

"What if we fail?" shouted Xizhu. "Do we carve an inscription that says we threw away our money and our lives for another dry hole in the ground?"

There was a burst of laughter following that remark.

"The tablet will record our failure too," Wangquan said through clenched teeth. "If we fail to reach water even with drills, it will be a warning for generations to come, that this is not a place to live. That we should abandon the village and go elsewhere."

Zhao Qiaoying leaped to her feet angrily.

"Just listen to you!" she cried. "Other communes invite Wangquan to advise them, but you place your trust in tricksters and necromancers from outside. Did you know he has written an article on his experiences, and it's right here." She waved a magazine at the crowd, and opening it, began to read aloud. The crowd listened, but the words were unfamiliar and the subject was way over their heads. Qiaoying snapped the magazine shut.

"It's no use. You wouldn't understand anyway. I won't waste words: I'm pledging a hundred yuan. You all say I won't stay in the village, and you might be right. What is it to me if you have to go fifteen and twenty li for water!"

The crowd was silenced by Qiaoying's tongue-lashing. They were impressed by Wangquan's article, though it meant little. But Qiaoying had become a celebrity of sorts since her bumper crop of peanuts and cotton last autumn proved that "scientific farming" worked. That stood for something.

The people were finally convinced, and noisy discussions began to find an equitable way of contributing.

Duan Xifeng caught Wangquan's eye. He knew she wanted to discuss pledging with him, but he made no move to join her. Nothing in the house belonged to him. Making a pledge would only lead to another row with Xifeng's mother. Xifeng's mother had threatened to drive him from the house once before. Actually he would welcome it, but he knew it was only an empty threat. Nothing would free him from the Duans. He thought of Qiaoying's support then, and he made up his mind to free himself, the sooner the better.

Seeing that her man was ignoring her, Xifeng went home alone. She knew how much the project meant to Wangquan, and she wanted to help. She thought about her own life: the marriage that was not a marriage. Something had to be done. The pledges were beginning to come in when Xifeng returned, followed by two boys carrying a sewing machine that was almost new. The crowd parted to make way for them. The youths carried the sewing machine to the front of the courtyard and put it down.

Xifeng spoke with a tremor in her voice.

"The well at Pine Creek was planned by my little Jing's father. We'd never be able to repay all of you if he fails. You've been generous in supporting him, and I too must do my share. Right now I am short of cash, but I do have this sewing machine. I pledge it in the name of little Jing's father. Even if the well fails, we will not leave this place. The next generation will carry on the work. By the time little Jing grows up, the four modernizations will be in place, and some day we will strike water. That too is my pledge."

There was a round of applause as she finished.

Wangquan bowed his head in confusion, surprised at the depth of Xifeng's understanding.

After that, those who did not have money went home and brought whatever they could lay their hands on. A continuous stream of people trudged back and forth along the cobbled streets. In no time the moonlit courtyard had turned into a fairground. There were bicycles, and sewing machines; coffins and coffin boards. Young women brought quilt covers, and fabrics they had put away for their weddings. Old women found antiques, old jewelry, silver coins and baskets of eggs. Every pledge was carefully recorded. It was a happy throng of people who saw the sufferings of countless generations coming to an end.

* * *

The autumn winds had begun, and the sorghum stood red and tall in the fields. At the bottom of the well the drill hummed day and night, boring closer and closer to the water table.

One evening Wangquan's family was ranged round a small table set under the shade of a birch tree, having their meal. It was a simple dinner. There was a bowl of cool vermicelli mixed with beans as a side dish. The main course was millet cooked with marrow and yams, flavored with vinegar, garlic sprouts and hot pepper oil. Xiuxiu was feeding her little black cat out of her bowl. Little Jing, who had begun to walk, leaned against his father's knee, gnawing a piece of yam. Xifeng talked of plans for after the harvest. She was hoping to buy another sewing machine when they had some spare cash.

Sanze, the tractor driver, came running just then.

"Come quick! The tractor's broke down, and there's not much water in the well."

Wangquan put down his bowl and asked, "How long will it take to fix the tractor?"

Sanze threw up his hands. "How should I know?"

Wangquan frowned, and when he spoke again, his voice was harsh. "Go to Sun Fuchang right now. Tell him the tractor broke down, and we need everybody in the village to carry water up there. If we stop pouring water down the well for just an hour and forty-five minutes, the sides could collapse." He turned to Xifeng then and said, "You go to my grandfather, tell him what happened and get him to help round up the people."

He filled two buckets, lashed them to a carrying pole, and went towards Pine Creek as fast as he could.

The gong rang out and the partly repaired loudspeakers crackled and blared through the gathering dusk. Soon the road to Pine Creek was clogged with carts, and men and women carrying buckets of water. Wangquan mingled with the crowd.

"Did someone fall in the well, or is there a house on fire?" someone asked.

"This is something quite new," another chimed in. "We're putting water in the well instead of taking it out."

Wangquan bowed his head and kept walking.

"Hey, have a rest."

Wangquan looked up and saw Qiaoying perched on the offending tractor. She threw him a tiny handkerchief. "Come to the other side of the tractor where nobody can see us."

Wangquan mopped his face with the handkerchief and handed it back.

"Sanze is trying to fix the tractor. What are you doing? Get a carrying pole and help, before somebody starts talking about you."

"Listen to him!" Qiaoying arched an eyebrow. "It will take hours for the man in the commune to find the right parts. So I suggested that Sanze find some used parts which might do for a short while. The sooner the tractor gets going the better for everybody."

"You're always right," Wangquan shifted his carrying pole to the other shoulder and moved on muttering, "The trouble with you is that you're soft. You haven't the spunk for hardship. Why, the time I carried stones . . . "

Qiaoying didn't wait for him to finish. She'd heard the story before. "You went a whole day without eating, and worked till you dropped." Qiaoying got off the tractor and blocked his way. "If I hear that story again, I'll puke. You want to see me work till I drop? All right; I'll show you."

Shortly afterwards Qiaoying appeared in the long line of water carriers wending their way to Pine Creek. She had changed into some shabby clothes, and shouldered a carrying pole from which two buckets of equal size were hung. People who recognized her tried to engage her in conversation. But the stony look on her face deterred them. After a few lame attempts, people left her alone. Wangquan tried to speak to her too, but she quickened her step and ignored him. Wangquan let her go, and grimly pressed on. At midnight, the brigade kitchen prepared rice gruel and pancakes, and everybody settled down to rest and eat. Qiaoying alone continued working, and Wangquan kept her company, not leaving her side for an instant.

Xifeng watched from a distance. Someone handed her a pancake but she was too upset to eat it. Instead she shredded it and gave it to one of the donkeys. She choked back her tears and melted into the line of water carriers.

Qiaoying's injured leg was throbbing. She limped badly, but she would not stop. On the contrary she pushed herself harder, determined to see how much she could endure. Wangquan, following her, begged her to stop. But she would not listen.

"Who are you to mind my business?" she barked.

As Qiaoying emptied her buckets into the storage tank, everything suddenly went black. She toppled unconscious into the mud puddles around the tank. Wangquan and some others carried her to dry ground and laid her down. It was a while before she came to. Seeing Wangquan anxiously squatting beside her, Qiaoying smiled weakly, "Now you've seen me work till I drop. I never want to hear your story again."

Wangquan nodded and smiled ruefully.

Qiaoying lay on the ground, her head resting on a stone. Overhead the moon was very bright.

"It's hard to work till you drop," she mused. "You're right about one thing though. I don't have the will to endure. But why should life be endured?"

"It's the way life is." replied Wangquan.

Qiaoying was very tired. She shifted her body into a more comfortable position. "But it shouldn't be. Let me lie here awhile. I'm so very tired " Her voice trailed off into sleep.

Wangquan took two padded coats from the tent nearby. He spread one on the grass and lifted her onto it. Then he covered her with the other. He wiped the sweat from her brow, and as he rose to leave, someone called him softly out of the darkness.

Sun Wanshui was squatting in front of the neat rows of stone samples waiting for him. "Have you got a smoke?"

Wangquan lit two cigarettes and handed one to his grandfather. They smoked in silence. The old man did not speak until half his cigarette was gone. He ran a hand along a pile of stone that hadn't yet been cataloged.

"Are these new?" he asked. "I think you've gone as deep as you should."

"Under this strata of impervious rock there's another formation that holds water," Wangquan said softly. "Besides we haven't reached the depth we planned yet."

"I don't understand the theories, but I know rocks. If you go through this layer and there's no water underneath, your water will drain away through the crack. Listen to me. Stop the drill and test if there's water before you go any further."

The storage tank was full and the water carriers had dispersed. The drill had already been shut down.

The apparatus for measuring the water level was a long metal tube with a capacity equal to sixteen buckets of water. The tube was lowered into the well and drawn up and the reading was jotted down. The water was poured off and the tube was lowered again. Three readings were taken. All three registered at 182.3 meters. Wangquan could not believe his eyes. He looked searchingly into the grease-smudged faces of his workmates, who grinned and thumped him on the back. Wangquan was suddenly lightheaded. He filled a canteen with water and walked a little unsteadily toward the old man squatting beside the piles of stone. His legs gave way, and he crashed to his knees in front of Wanshui. Wangquan buried his head against the old man's chest, sobbing.

Wanshui held him as tenderly as a child, murmuring, "Your grandfather's old. You mustn't frighten him like this!"

Wangquan was trembling all over. He pressed his face against his grandfather, and finally gasped out, "We've struck water!"

As the meaning of those words slowly sank in, Sun Wanshui seemed to sag. Tears ran down his furrowed face and into his wispy beard. He took the canteen from Wangquan, stood and faced in the direction of the old graveyard, and emptied the canteen onto the ground. Then half muttering and half chanting he called on the spirits of his ancestors to bear witness to the night's happenings.

"Father . . . rest in peace . . . Fugui, my son . . . rest in peace. Man needs earth and water to live. Now we have both."

Wangquan stood beside his grandfather, his grimy face streaked with tears. He wanted to wake Qiaoying but she slept so peacefully he didn't have the heart to rouse her.

The sky was turning light. The mountains were a misty green silhouetted against the firmament. Dew drops glistened like pearls in Qiaoying's long black hair. A wild violet, peeping out from under her sleeve, trembled in the breeze.

* * *

Half a month later, a girl of twelve died suddenly in Du Valley, fifteen li away. Sun Fuchang paid the sum of a hundred and fifty yuan to have the girl buried beside Sun Wangcai. Thus the youth who craved love and warmth in life found a wife in the netherworld.

On the day of the burial Sun Fuchang got on his bicycle and went into the city on an errand. At dusk, on his way home, he stopped at the old graveyard and stood a moment before the graves of his son and daughter-in-law.

The sorghum was tall and red in the fields. Patches of wild chrysanthemums lit the pale green of the Taihang mountains. And the maples blazed red and gold.

Chapter 12

The gold and crimson leaves of maple and poplar rustled in the chill wind of late autumn.

One brisk evening a small crowd jammed into Qiaoying's house. They had come to see the new black-and-white television that Qiaoying bought with money earned from selling her corn on the free market in the city. That so much money could be made from a tiny scrap of land on the river bank was the talk of the village. People came not only to watch the "little cinema" but to beg a handful of superior grade corn seeds. Before long every square inch of space was occupied. In such a crowd one can expect mishaps. A window pane was broken, a curtain got torn, and the kang was trampled. But Qiaoying and her mother did not seem to mind. They greeted everyone with a smile, and cigarettes were passed around as though it were a festival.

At seven o'clock, Qiaoying switched on the television. All eyes were glued to the square of flickering bluish light. Black lines zigzagged across the screen and though Qiaoying turned the knobs this way and that, no images appeared. But the set worked perfectly when she tried it in the store. Perhaps her watch was fast, she told the crowd. The set was turned off, and more cigarettes were passed around. A while later the television was turned on again, and again only black zig-zag lines appeared. Wangquan asked Qiaoying for the manual which he scanned quickly.

"The mountains are cutting off the reception," he said.

The disappointed crowd quickly dispersed. Only a few young people remained. Someone suggested asking the commune to set up an antenna.

"We had to do a lot of lobbying, but that's how we got the cultural center," Wangquan said optimistically.

"Oh, yes. And what's in it? Chess, a few decks of cards, and a few magazines. Why they had a library in the city during the Qing dynasty!"

Wangquan pondered the problem a moment, picked up the television and started out the door.

"Let's try it on top of Qinglong mountain!"

The young people, armed with extension cables, clamps and a few simple tools carried the television set to a high ridge. The supply line to the village ran along the ridge strung between poles. The television set was attached to a long extension, and someone climbed a pole and connected it to a wire. The set was turned on again, still only dots and dashes appeared.

All around the mountains rose waves of blue and mauve, stretching as far as the eye could see. Wangquan drew a deep breath. The mountains seemed to press in on him squeezing the life out of him, swallowing him. There was no telling which particular peak was blocking the reception. There were too many. Far below, the lights of Old Well Village looked pathetically insignificant.

Qiaoying gazed about her gloomily. The trees and flowers and rocks so familiar in the daylight had melted into darkness. The mountains rose all around her like towering waves on a black and angry sea about to swamp the little patch of ground she stood on. She shuddered and hurried down the path.

Wangquan told Xizhu to carry the television and equipment home, and hurried to catch up with Qiaoying. They walked side by side without a word. Beyond a bend in the path was a small clump of poplars and maples. Qiaoying took Wangquan's hand and drew him down into the shadows. Their arms went around each other, and in the darkness, they kissed; long, searching kisses that sent the blood thundering through their bodies. Wangquan felt himself come alive again. Every nerve and fiber in him tingled. Yet somewhere in the back of his mind there was a nagging premonition of disaster.

There was a rustling in the bushes behind them. Qiaoying gave a startled cry and buried her face against his chest. His arms tightened about her.

"It's nothing. Just some small animal," he comforted.

A fox and her cub broke from the underbrush and darted across the clearing.

"Why, it was your friend the fox," Wangquan said teasingly.

"I don't like them any more. They frighten me."

"Ah, maybe you're not a fox fairy after all."

"They say that the sorceress has been casting spells again. But I didn't feel anything."

"You've been with humans too long."

She snuggled against him, seeking his warmth.

"You've warmed me with your body," she said.

Afterwards, she ran a languid hand through her hair, and her eyes were deep and peaceful.

"I'm leaving. Go with me. We'll go as far away from here as we can."

"But what will you do?"

She sensed his hesitancy, and she went cold.

"The new policy allows me to do all sorts of things. Study new agricultural techniques, develop new crops, market research. Don't you worry about me." She sounded cold, but in her heart there was still a sliver of hope.

"Qiaoqiao, I don't know how to say this, but I do love you," Wangquan began lamely. He told her then about the letter from Geologist Sun. His article in the *Water Resources Journal* had impressed many experts. So much so that some were of the opinion that it could become the starting point of new discoveries. But it required more research and more experimentation.

"I feel I have a responsibility to try and solve the problem of water shortage."

Qiaoying did not let him finish.

"You sure have a lot of responsibilities. There's your wife and your son. You're secretary of the village, and now this water business. Thank heaven I won't be a burden to you."

Wangquan was silent. Qiaoying continued almost cheerily. She had been to the commune offices a few days earlier intending to make some discreet inquiries about divorce procedures. Secretary Li had shown her a map of the Taihang Mountains and told her that the state planned to reforest the whole area and to reduce agriculture. It has been proven that these mountains only became barren after the forests had been destroyed.

"Reestablish the forests, and the climate will change, and there'll be water again. We've gone a full circle round to where our ancestors started a thousand years ago," Qiaoying said.

Wangquan shook his head. He did not understand any of it. He felt like a drowning man clutching at straws.

"Our ancestors had to cut down the forests to grow food or starve. Just as we have to sink wells to go on living until the forests grow."

"You've always got a reason," Qiaoying sighed and stood up. She picked a red maple leaf and gave it to him. "People in Beijing call it the symbol of love. If it's really so, then these mountains can be full of love."

"Qiaoqiao," Wangquan asked, "if you don't want to stay, why did you do all this scientific farming in these two years?"

"Not because I want to stay," Qiaoying said calmly. "I did it to test myself, to see what I could accomplish. Now I've got confidence. I can do anything I want to. It's time for me to go."

She dusted herself off, and made her way down the path without glancing back. The mist was rising. Wangquan did not follow her but walked back up the mountain. Patches of dank white mist drifted through trees, rocks, bushes and grass, changing them into strange, ghostly shapes. He had become a lost soul, wandering this haunted place where everything was vague and indistinct. It's time to leave, he told himself over and over. Qiaoying would leave and the bond of love and desire would be cut forever. He staggered on blindly, unconsolable, almost insane from loss. Suddenly the earth gave way under him, and a great blackness crashed down around him.

He woke up on a jumble of brambles and rotting weeds at the bottom of a pit. Wangquan had fallen into one of the countless dry wells that dotted the mountainside. He lay there, still dazed.

Above, through the drifting mist he could make out the inky sky beyond. There were no stars. Yet the sky is full of stars, he thought, and each star, a separate world. How many worlds there must be. And how vast. But Old Well was all the world he would ever know.

The night was cold, and he was covered with dew. The cold was slowly seeping into him. His limbs grew heavy and stiff. He felt as if he were slowly turning into stone.

He lifted his head and screamed, "Mountain!"

There was no echo, the sound of his voice swallowed by the night.

He screamed again, with all the strength he could gather, "Well!"

No echo came back to him, only a strange buzzing in his ears. This must be a nightmare, he thought, and shouted again,

"Man!"

The sound started a trickle of sand, then silence closed in on him again. He started talking to himself aloud:

"I remember now . . . Things rotting in pits produce gases that kill . . . That's why I'm cold . . . and dizzy . . . and I can't breathe . . . Got to get out . . . get out!" He crawled on his hands and knees and felt around the sides of the pit looking for a foothold. Slowly he pulled himself up, clinging to roots and crevices between the rough stones.

The pit was not deep but it seemed an eternity before he reached the top. He sprawled on the grass, gasping. The cold air cleaned his mind and everything was clear again.

Wangquan's grandfather and Sun Fuchang had promised not to stand in the way of his leaving once the well was dug. Now the well was a reality, but he had lost the will to leave. He was still moved by the ideal of helping his struggling people. And there was his son, growing up in a miserable village, in a home without love. Yes, he could have love and freedom and Qiaoying, but without a purpose, a cause. He was torn between the two, for there could be no compromise. In the end, though, he knew he could not turn his back on ideals and his homeland. Generations had drawn strength from their visions and this parched land to struggle on. He had to do the same.

At first light, Wanglai came to summon Wangquan to their

grandfather's house. When Wangquan arrived, Qiaoying was already seated in the room. She was dressed for traveling, and her knapsack stood on the floor beside her. His grandfather sat cross-legged on the kang, puffing on his water pipe and coughing. The old man did not seem to notice Wangquan. When the coughing spell passed, he spoke to Qiaoying hoarsely. "Your father left for a few years, but he came back in 1960. Nowadays, with the new policy of responsibility, things are changing all the time. You don't have to leave."

Qiaoying bowed her head.

"I want to make something out of my life. And I'm not my father. I will never come back."

" 'Never' is a long time. Wangquan's third uncle has been away for years. He's an important cadre now, but he's coming back soon. Don't turn your back on your home and the people who love you."

"He's coming back to do honor to his ancestors. I'll come back too, some day, when I've made something of myself. But now, I want to live."

"There's some truth in that," the old man muttered. He reached into the little black wood cupboard that stood in the corner of the kang, and brought out a little packet wrapped in brown paper. He tore off the brown paper, and inside was a square of blue silk wrapped around a pot shard.

"This has been in our family for many generations," said the old man, handing the pot shard to Qiaoying. "I want you to have it, to remind you in times of trouble that there will always be refuge here for you." His eyes went from Qiaoying to Wangquan. "I'm sorry I spoiled things for you. I will regret that for the rest of my life. But in my heart you have always been my granddaughter-in-law."

Qiaoying accepted the pot shard, and bowed solemnly.

"I must go now, grandfather," she said simply, and quickly left the room.

That one word, "grandfather," stabbed Sun Wanshui to the quick. He clenched his teeth, determined to hold back the tears, but he could not.

* * *

The streets were deserted, except for a few dogs slinking by. Wangquan and Qiaoying walked in silence. There was nothing left to say between them.

Somewhere a cock crowed. The breeze coming off the fields was laden with the greenish smell of cow dung. Behind a wall was a clash of buckets, as someone prepared to carry water from the deep well at Pine Creek. The tufts of grass sprouting in between roof tiles were tinted purple in the early light. A few red apples and golden persimmons reached their branches over a wall, trembling with drops of dew, like a mysterious dream: the beauty of Old Well, a native land that people love and hate at the same time. The red Iron Bull Model 55 tractor parked at the end of the Blue Stone Bridge. Qiaoying said something to Sanze, who was filling the water tank and was about to start the engine. Then she walked to the bridge with Wangquan on the road toward the county seat. As they were crossing the bridge, Wangquan heard the water flowing over the rocks and suddenly felt that Qiaoying was like the pure, clear stream of the river, roaring out of the mountain, a force nothing could resist. He was a heavy and solid mountain, who stood there to watch the stream pour toward a vast, far world. Climbing up a long slope and reaching the graveyard, Wangquan grasped a handful of wet soil and wrapped it in his handkerchief and handed it to Qiaoying. Untying the wrapping, Qiaoying spread the soil on the side of the road. Fighting tears and trying to hide her feelings, she said with a bitter smile, "I don't need a handful of soil to remember this place. My blood has been shed into the soil and the blood in my body is mixed with yours and the young people's in our village. Isn't that enough? How could I forget our village? Brother Wangquan, I cannot wait for you all my life because I'm a woman. A woman is expected to be married. But until I die, I will never forget the times we were together. There are so many people in the world, but we were the best together. Here's the pot shard—please keep it because it has been in the Sun family for generations. It's not right for me to keep the token of your Sun family ancestory. Now that I'm leaving, our secret is finished and I will never be back." With a roar of the engine, the Iron Bull 55 climbed up the long slope. Don't see me off any more, please," Qiaoying said as she stopped, seeing a small figure like a shadow standing on the ridge of Sleeping Tiger Mountain. "Xifeng is watching from there, and from now on you should treat her better than before. She was very kind and I knew how much I was hurting her." The tractor parked two meters in front of them and the driver Sanze stepped on the gas and waited. However, he dared not turn his head to catch a glimpse of the scene behind him. "It's time for me to go. Let's shake hands. We never did that before." Qiaoying took a deep breath before she stretched out her hand. The grief could be seen on his thin, long face. He said nothing, but grit his teeth instead of stretching out his hand. Qiaoying did not want to leave him, but with a regretful smile turned her head, stalked toward the tractor and jumped on it quickly. As the tractor drove away, Sun Wangquan knew he had lost Qiaoying and their love forever. He wanted to cry and felt that his heart and lungs would explode, but he clenched his teeth and stayed silent. Like a blend of lava and blood, the mixed feelings of solitude, grief, uncertainty and depression pushed from inside him with terrifying force. But he knew it would only be a cry of insanity, and these feelings remained locked in him. He would always remember the unvoiced pain, the crying that was not crying.

The mountains echoed with the noise of the tractor. In a moment it appeared again beyond a grove of maples. It moved with an obscene swiftness, oblivious to the pain of parting.

From his vantage point, the whole graveyard lay at his feet. In the days of the "Great Leap Forward" and the "Study Camps" many of the graves were destroyed, but their ruins could still be seen, laid out in the shape of a fan. Across the river, the village lay in deep blue shadow. Already wisps of smoke were rising from chimneys, drifting in a milky haze over the rooftops. There is life down there, he thought.

His fingers closed around the pot shard she had handed him at the last moment. Her words came back to him now, sharp and clear: "It belongs to you . . . it's a part of your life . . . "

He looked at the tumbled graves, the village, and the fragment of an ancient pot and sensed his roots. Roots that went so deep that nothing would budge them.

The tractor was almost out of sight now. He scrambled up one more ridge, and another, straining to keep it in view. The tractor had reached the highway that followed the loops of the river. In another moment it rounded a bend and was gone.

The sun was climbing past the mountain tops.

The mountains rose all around him in long waves of blue and purple. The wind filled his nostrils with the heady smell of goat dung, wild chrysanthemums and nameless herbs, and through the soles of his feet, he felt the pulse of the earth.

He started back down the mountain again.

Below, beside the Qinglong River, was the village half hidden by smoke.

But he knew it was all there. And his son, and a good woman. And memories.

Yes, there would always be memories.

About the Translator

Born in Beijing, David Kwan is a Eurasian who grew up in a multilingual household, with Chinese and English as his first languages. The family left before Liberation (1949) and it was not until the late 1980s that he returned to his native city.

Indicative of his bicultural background is the fact that one of his favorite recollections is reading a Chinese translation of Defoe's *Robinson Crusoe* at age six. As a child, he passed the time by translating stories from English into Chinese and vice versa. His earliest literary influences were his tutors and writers Lin Yu Tang and Pearl S. Buck, who were friends of his parents.

Kwan has been a social worker and a broadcaster, but most of his career has been in the airline and travel industries. He is the author of radio scripts, short stories, travel articles, plays and textbooks. Since 1987 he has divided his time between his home in Canada and Beijing, where he has taught English at at the University of International Business and Economics. During this period he also translated five modern Chinese novels, including the present volume, more than a dozen short stories and two plays.

When not in China, he lives with his sons in Vancouver, British Columbia. He is currently writing a historical novel on the life of Chinshihuang and continuing his translations of modern Chinese literature.

Glossary

A*gricultural Study Campaign*—This refers to the period of the so-called "learning from Dazhai in agriculture." Dazhai, a production brigade in Xiyang County, Shanxi Province, was heralded as a pacesetter of China's agriculture in 1964 when Premier Zhou Enlai delivered his report on the work of the government at the First Session of the Third National People's Congress. Before the Cultural Revolution, Dazhai was indeed a good model in agriculture, excelling in productivity and self-reliance. Promoted across the country, the basic experiences of Dazhai did play a positive role in rural development. But in its later development, especially during the Cultural Revolution, Dazhai was gradually transformed into its opposite, becoming finally a model of "Left" errors.

Ah Q—Ah Q is the main character in *The True Story of Ah Q*, a well-known story by Lu Xun, one of modern China's greatest writers. This story was written in 1921, set in the China of 1911, during the period of the democratic revolution. It is the tragedy of Ah Q, an impoverished peasant who suffers humiliation, beatings and persecution, dreams vaguely of revolution and ends up being executed at the whim of the authorities. Ah Q's servile attitudes were formed by the feudal ruling class which exploits and oppresses him. The abuse which Ah Q passively accepts makes him unable to resist or even understand the evils of contemporary society. But, while revealing Ah Q's weakness of will, the author shows deep sympathy for his plight. It was Lu Xun's hope that the broad masses of peasants, victims of feudal oppression and imperialist aggression, might be aroused and made aware of the causes of their suffering.

Anti-Japanese War—On July 7, 1937, Japanese forces attacked Lugouqiao (Marco Polo Bridge), to the southwest of Beiping (today's Beijing), and Chinese defenders retaliated. This has been known as the Lugouqiao Incident, which marked the beginning of Japan's all-out aggression against China and of China's War of Resistance Against Japan. One of the major military encounters in Asia, it continued as part of World War II, with the Chinese battling until the end of the war. On August 8, 1945, the Soviet Union declared war on Japan, and its Red Army attacked the Japanese aggressors in China's northeastern provinces. Meanwhile, the people's army in China counterattacked on a grand scale. On August 14, Japan surrendered unconditionally. On September 2, it signed the instrument of surrender. The Chinese people, after eight years of bitter struggle, finally won victory in the anti-Japanese war.

Branch Secretary—Head of a branch, the grassroots unit of the Communist Party.

cadre—A government-employed official or staff member.

catty—Or *jin,* a unit of weight equal to half a kilogram, used in China and Southeast Asian countries.

Chief of Security—Head of the Public Security Bureau of the county, equivalent to the police station in the United States.

commune, brigade—In 1958, Communist Party Chairman Mao Zedong called on agricultural cooperatives to form communes in which the individual peasant's land and tools were all owned by the commune. Rural people's communes were organized on a large scale in many provinces and autumonous regions. By

October 1958, the movement covered the entire country, with the exception of Tibet. Altogether, 26,425 people's communes were reportedly set up, embracing 121.94 million farmer households, or 98 percent of the total rural population. Three-level ownership (by the commune, the production brigade and the production team), with the production team as the basic unit, became the basic system of administration for the people's communes. After the Thirteenth National People's Congress held in 1986, the people's commune was replaced by the township. The brigades still function as working units.

County Brigade—A professional brigade of well construction under the Irrigation Bureau of the County. All the workers are employed by the government and get paid by month.

County Secretary of the Party—Head of the county-level Communist Party unit, in charge of the Party's daily work in the county.

County Committee—The organizational unit of the Communist Party at county level.

Dragon King—In Chinese mythology, the Dragon King was a god under the rule of the Jade Emperor, ordered to be in charge of the rain. He lived in his palace under the sea. As in *Old Well,* people historically built temples for the Dragon King where they worshiped him and prayed for rain.

Fen River—Flowing across central Shanxi Province, the Fen River is about 695 kilometers long and is the second largest tributary of the Yellow River, with great variation in flow, and large amounts of silt.

food allowance—The money people are allotted to bring up a child.

Four Modernizations— This term refers to the modernizations of industry, agriculture, national defense and science and technology being carried out in China. It was first initiated by the late Premier Zhou Enlai at the Fourth National People's Congress held in January 1975. It was reaffirmed by the Twelfth National Congress of the Communist Party of China in 1982.

Great Leap Forward—The "Great Leap Forward" and the movement to form rural people's communes were recklessly launched in 1957–58 under the influence of "Leftist" ideas at that time. The "Great Leap Forward" designated steel production as the key link and launched the movement to rapidly set up people's communes all over the country. Unfortunately, the effort was marred by many "Left" abuses and excesses, including incompetent direction, hastily and shoddily organized manufacturing, political posturing and opportunism. While much construction did occur, there was also enormous waste, useless steel production, and massive crop failures. The methods of organization were too unwieldy, and planning was often too arbitrary or based on inadequate technical knowledge.

kang—A heatable brick bed, kept warm by a fire contained inside the structure. It is commonly seen in north China.

li—A Chinese unit of length, equal to half a kilometer.

Loess—Bounded by the Qinling Mountains and the Weihe Plain in the south, the Great Wall in the north, the Taihang Mountains in the east and the Taohe River and Wuxiao Mountains in the west, it includes the entire Shanxi Province, northern Shaanxi, the greater part of Ningxia, central and eastern Gansu and western Henan. Covering 400,000 square kilometres and rising 800 to 2,000 metres above sea level, it is the third largest plateau of China. The Yellow River and its tributaries—the Taohe, Weihe and Luohe rivers—all flow across the Loess Plateau.

marriage settlement—The custom of requiring betrothal gifts from the bridegroom to the bride's family as part of the marriage agreement.

One is Best—This refers to China's population policy, which is a program to contain the birth rate by encouraging and actively supporting the practice of family planning. Each family is encouraged to have only one child.

Policy of responsibility—A contract responsibility system based on the household and linking remuneration to actual output, was put forward in 1979 as a new form of socialist collective economy, a creation by Chinese farmers under the leadership of the Communist Party. It is quite different from the previous model of "all eat from the same pot," where extreme egalitarianism meant that there was little connection between a farmer's personal productivity and the amount of compensation received. It is not, however, intended by the Party to become a totally private economy of isolated small-scale individual households. Rather, the hope has been that the advantages of collective effort and the incentive of the individuals would be combined, thus making possible a so-called "development of socialist agriculture with Chinese characteristics." The *contract* responsibility system refers to the system of fixing production quotas for individual households.

Qianmen—At the south of the Tiananmen Square is Qianmen, or "Front Gate," the double gate-tower that in former times connected the northern and southern parts of the city. Now Qianmen has become a busy commercial district.

Qinglong River—A local river in Shanxi Province.

Republic—The revolution of 1911 demolished the age-old imperial system but failed to establish a popular, democratic government in its place. The Republic it founded under the provisional presidency of Dr. Sun Yat-sen was dominated from the first by a Manchu general, Yuan Shikai. After his death, the country was split between rival warlords, encouraged and financed by rival foreign powers. Unity was briefly restored by Chiang Kai-shek's reformed Republican Party, the Kuomintang, which won control of most of China in 1928. Chiang's regime lasted about twenty years. In 1949, the People's Liberation Army swept through China from Beijing to the southern coast, and on October 1 the People's Republic of China was officially founded by the revolutionaries.

Secretary of the Commune—Head of the commune-level Communist Party unit, in charge of the Party's daily work of the commune.

Taihang Mountains—Running northeast-southwest, the Taihang Mountains cross the Shanxi Plateau and Hebei Plain, 1,500 to 2,000 meters above sea level. The main peak is Mount Lesser Wutai with an elevation of 2,870 meters.

Wangfujing—A commercial street in downtown Beijing.

yuan—The monetary unit of China, presently equal to about 30 US cents.

New Chinese Fiction

Lapse of Time

WANG ANYI

NEW CHINESE FICTION!

—From the Most Popular Woman Writer in Shanghai

"In these wonderful stories, Wang Anyi has done even more than create a vivid gallery of how some human beings intensely lived through years of enormous upheaval . . . Through the magic of art, she has enmeshed us in these lives and carried us into understanding the circumstances, humanity, pain, and promise of those years."

—Tillie Olsen—
—author of TELL ME A RIDDLE—

"Intimate, well-observed collection of short fiction. . . a solid addition to the growing body of Chinese literature on the Cultural Revolution."

—Kirkus Reviews —

"Now that the Cultural Revolution is over and Chinese books are available to American readers, I would recommend Lapse of Time as a good place to begin."

—Maxine Hong Kingston—
—author of THE WOMAN WARRIOR—

LAPSE OF TIME
by Wang Anyi

Short stories by a young woman who represents the new generation in China today. She writes of young people whose lives were disrupted by the Cultural Revolution, or who struggle with the new practical realities of Deng Xiaoping's China. They are searching for new lives, new values . . . and new ways of writing.

China Books, 1988. 224 pp.

ISBN 0-8351-2031-7 . . . . cloth $16.95
ISBN 0-8351-2032-5 . . . . paper $8.95

Send for our mail-order catalog for a complete listing of books from and about China